DATE DUE			
FEB 2 7 '11			
FEB 2 1 2012			
MAY 2 9 2012			
8/16/19			

Believing in Hope

Yasmin Peace Series Book 2

Stephanie Perry Moore

MOODY PUBLISHERS

CHICAGO

© 2009 by
STEPHANIE PERRY MOORE

All Scripture quotations are taken from the King James Version.

Editor: Kathryn Hall
Interior Design: Ragont Design
Cover Design and Photography: Trevell Southhall at TS Design Studios

Library of Congress Cataloging-in-Publication Data

Moore, Stephanie Perry.
    Believing in hope / Stephanie Perry Moore.
        p. cm. — (Yasmin Peace series ; bk. 2)
    Summary: As family tensions and school unrest soar, eighth-grade triplet Yasmin relies on her faith and, through a new club at school, discovers that there is hope on the other side of every obstacle, even for those living in the projects.
    ISBN 978-0-8024-8603-5
    [1. Family problems—Fiction. 2. Christian life—Fiction. 3. Clubs—Fiction. 4. Middle schools—Fiction. 5. Schools—Fiction. 6. African Americans—Fiction. 7. Triplets—Fiction. 8. Brothers and sisters—Fiction.] I. Title. 10-194
PZ7.M788125Bel 2009   Moody
[Fic]--dc22   (Ana.)
                            1/10
                            $6.99   2008037267

1 3 5 7 9 10 8 6 4 2

Printed in the United States of America

Dedicated to
The Young Ladies of L.I.G.H.T.
(a mentoring program at Kendrick Middle School
in Clayton County, Georgia)

Forever believe in God's goodness,
though your world is tough.
I pray you and all who read this title
know that in hoping for change,
change is going to come!
Believe that!

Contents

Chapter 1

Stronger Each Day

Yasmin, you and your brothers need to come over to my house right now," Myrek said to me over the phone with great urgency in his voice.

"Huh? What are you talking about?" I said to my next door neighbor and best buddy of many years.

I was really confused about why he sounded panicked. My mom had just come back from Myrek's apartment. Mr. Mike, Myrek's dad, had asked her to come over to discuss the situation about Jada, Myrek's sister. My brother Jeffery Jr., whom everybody called Jeff, used to date Jada. Well, now Jada says that she is pregnant—and that Jeff is the father!

Though my tough brother York wasn't at all happy about it, my smart brother Yancy and I certainly thought this was great news. I wasn't naïve or anything. I know that it is not God's plan for a teenage girl to be pregnant. But because of what my grandma, Big Mama, always said could come out of a mess, I had hope that

God will bring a miracle into these circumstances. After explaining the situation to my brothers and me, Mom realized that she'd left her Bible at Myrek's house, so she went back to get it.

"Yas, please don't ask me no questions. Seriously, could y'all come on over here?" Myrek said as I heard loud talking behind him.

My mom was over there cutting up. Why though? She had just said that we needed to be prayerful and God would work everything out. It had only been months since Jeff took his own life. Just when I was getting over the fact that I would probably lose every connection I ever had with him, I find out that I will have a niece or nephew, keeping a part of Jeff in this world. What could possibly be going wrong now?

Quickly, I slid on my slippers and hung up the phone without saying bye.

I looked at York and Yancy. "Let's go. Mom's over there showing out."

"I told y'all this isn't our fight. This isn't our business," York said, not wanting to get up out of his seat. "Jada is too young to have a baby. Besides, whatever that girl wants to do with her body ain't got nothing to do with us."

"Yeah. Like Jeffery would want her to kill the baby?" Yancy said to York. "We gotta be his voice. We gotta do whatever we can to make sure she knows that she's not in this alone. So get up and let's go over there. Now!"

I couldn't believe Yancy grabbed York's collar. I knew that wasn't going to go over well. The two of them started pushing and shoving each other back and forth. It was just killing me how every five minutes they were getting into it about something.

"Guys, this isn't about us. Mom is over there fussing with

Myrek's dad. Can't we just keep whatever we feel to ourselves and go bring Mama home?"

York said, "Mama's grown. What about this don't you understand?"

"I understand that she's our mom and obviously it's a big enough deal that Myrek thought we could help by being over there. It's not like I'm putting my nose into something that I'm supposed to stay out of. We were basically asked to come over and help. If you want to sit here and do nothing, or if you two want to stay here and argue, then fine. I'll go by myself." I opened our apartment door and stood in the doorway with my body facing right.

"I'll go," York said, knowing that I made a very valid point.

The front door of Myrek's apartment was wide open.

"You just can't go around giving no demands, Yvette," Mr. Mike said to our mom. "Jada is my daughter. She's going to do what is best for her. All of us are struggling in these projects. We're barely able to take care of the kids we got now. You workin' two jobs. I'm working seventeen hours.

"How we gonna be able to take care of a grandchild? And your son ain't even here to help. I'm sorry if this hurts. I'm sorry if I'm saying the tough stuff, but I'm being real. Jeff's gone and we need to move on. Jada has a future that includes finishing school. And having a baby just ain't a part of that future."

My brothers and I were standing behind our mom.

"You not gon' tell me that y'all gon' deal with this without me!" Mom said, fussing. "Are you tellin' me that she's not gonna have the baby?"

Finally, he said, "Y'all need to get your mom up on out of my apartment. This is my daughter and we gon' deal with it how she needs to."

No one seemed to notice that Jada was in the corner crying. Our parents just kept going back and forth at it. They were getting so loud and crazy that obviously this girl could not take anymore of it. Suddenly, she ran outside and I followed her.

"Jeffery, why'd you have to leave me? I'm sorry I told you it was Bone's baby. I just thought it would be better. I didn't want to mess you up and keep you from going on to college. I didn't know you were gonna take it so hard. Please forgive me, God. Please forgive me!" Jada sobbed.

I was going out there to console Jada, but hearing what she said made me stop as if I'd come to a stop sign and a policeman was waiting to give me a ticket if I proceeded. And then when I was able to move, when I could go forward to comfort her, it was like my car broke down. How could I comfort a girl who basically was confessing to the fact that she was probably the reason why my brother took his own life?

Now granted, I found out that he owed Bone money for not throwing the high school state championship game. I'd also learned that his grades were horrible and he probably wasn't going to get a chance to go to college after all. But I still knew Jeff to be so strong. None of that made me think he'd be that down. But this? I believe that he loved Jada. If she told him that she was having someone else's baby, he would have been devastated. I screamed to release my pent-up frustration.

Jada turned around and said, "How long have you been standing there?"

"Long enough," I said with one hand on my hip. "Why'd you lie to my brother?" I demanded.

"I don't know. I thought I was doing the right thing. I thought I could pull this off. I didn't think he would end everything. I was fooling myself that Jeff wouldn't care. Please, please forg—"

Getting close to her face, I snarled and said, "Please what? My brother's gone. We don't have no real reasons or answers why he did what he did. If you told him this terrible lie, then of course he felt helpless and weak. How could you? And you don't even know if you want the baby!"

Jada looked at me with tears streaming down her face and said, "Yasmin, you have no clue about what I'm going through!"

I was overcome with the sick feeling grief brings. At that point, I ran back to my own apartment. Sitting on the bed that I shared with my mom, all I could do was rock back and forth.

Lord, I thought I knew You were there. You've proven to me that You care about me, but why does each day seem to be harder? Why can't I just feel good? Why can't I just get good news? Why can't I be a normal eighth-grade girl? Drama free?

≈◊≈

"Wait a minute. I'm not taking no handouts from nobody. What's all this food for?" I heard Mom say in an irate way.

I was surprised to see my counselor and pastor's wife, Mrs. Newman, and my English teacher, Miss Bennett, at our apartment. They said they had come on behalf of the *Reach Out and Touch* ministry from our church. The baskets of food they brought sure smelled good. So good that my brothers had come out of their bedroom to find out what was happening.

"Mom, what you sayin'? We hungry," York said to her as his eyes got really wide, staring at all of the food.

"Boy, I told you, you might be getting bigger but you are not grown up in here. I didn't ask for no handouts. I don't want no handouts. Thank y'all very much, but go to somebody else's house. The lady next door on the left, Sandra, got two little kids. And believe it or not, she's struggling worse than me. Take the food to her."

"Mom!" I said, feeling really embarrassed that my mother had such pride. My grandma had fussed at her about being too prideful to accept help. She couldn't even accept a blessing.

The first time that we visited the church, Pastor Newman's message moved my whole family and we joined the church. Then the minister over the new members' ministry explained to us the importance of not only being a member but of having a relationship with Jesus Christ. Mom even left the service saying that she was happier than she'd been in a long while.

"Mom, how come we can't accept it?" I asked.

"Because—in case you forgot, Yasmin Peace, I'm the one who makes decisions up in here," she said sharply.

They were being nice to us and bringing us a meal when, truth be told, earlier in the day Mom was trying to figure out what we were gonna eat. I could understand not wanting to take handouts if you didn't need it, but she'd already said we were struggling. She had two jobs and was still behind on the rent and utilities. Coupled with the way my brothers ran through the food stamps, we needed help.

Mrs. Newman said, "You know, I'm sorry, Mrs. Peace. The church wasn't trying to make you feel like you can't do this. We know you didn't ask for a handout. It's just that this is the end of the holiday season and we'd like to bless grieving families who have suffered a severe loss. This is just a little something to start the New Year off with a victory."

Miss Bennett stepped forward and said, "Yes, she's right. So many people get so much during the time when they actually lose a loved one, but after that, sometimes they still need folks to come by and show them some love. That's what we're all about."

Mrs. Newman chimed back in and said, "We can imagine the holidays had to be tough, but we were praying for you guys. If you need anything, the church is here to help. Please take this ham, fried chicken, green beans, rice, macaroni and cheese—"

"Aw, come on, Ma. You gotta let us get that," York said.

"Shut up, boy!" she said to him. "Go sit down."

"And we've got black-eyed peas," Mrs. Newman continued. "Can't start the New Year off without black-eyed peas. If you prefer us to take this food next door to your neighbor, we can do that. But we'd certainly love to give it to you all. Maybe you can invite your neighbors over here to share with you. There's plenty enough."

Mom looked at my brothers who were practically drooling like they couldn't wait to tear into the food. Then she looked over at me and saw that I was a little salty because she had sort of embarrassed me in front of our visitors.

Then she said calmly, "Just so you know, this isn't a handout. We appreciate it. Kids, let's put everything in the kitchen."

We laid the spread on the kitchen table. My brothers were smiling from our place in Jacksonville all the way to Miami.

Before Mrs. Newman and Miss Bennett left, they asked if we could circle up in prayer and thank God for His many blessings. My mom said that was a great idea; my brothers, who acted as if they hadn't eaten in years, reluctantly grabbed hands.

We walked over to the table and Mom just hugged me. "Thank you, baby," she said as she gave me a kiss on my forehead.

"For what?" I said still having a slight attitude.

"Just because. Just because," was all that she said.

Maybe I did need to keep trusting God. Maybe He was working in my mom's heart after all. Though I was still so bummed out with her, I had to force a smile on my face because of her change of heart. It sure felt good having her arms around me. Something was definitely working.

⤛❦⤜

"Ooh, this sure is a lot of food," Mom said after Mrs. Newman and Miss Bennett left. "Yas, why don't you go next door and see if Miss Sandra is at home."

"Yes, ma'am," I said and headed to her apartment. As I approached the door, I didn't even have to knock; I could tell there was no one home because it was so quiet. Usually, you could hear the kids playing and making noise inside their apartment. Besides, her car wasn't parked outside in its usual spot.

Miss Sandra was an interesting character. She had two young kids: a five-year-old daughter, Randi, and a son, Dante, who was almost two. She worked at the grocery store stocking items on the shelf, and she also worked nights at a second job.

Back last spring, I remember when she and my mom got into it. Mom had caught her leaving the kids at home alone while she was out trying to make ends meet. When Mom threatened to call the Department of Children and Family Services, also known as DCF, Miss Sandra just broke down. Ever since then, my mom was trying to do all she could to help the lady. We watched the kids, and we shared our food with them.

But after Jeff died, Mom just shut out all that helping others. One day I heard her mumbling that she could barely help her own children. How was she going to help someone else raise theirs? After that, we didn't know who was taking care of her little babies, but I knew my mom still cared about them.

"They're not there, Ma," I said, coming back to our apartment. Then she put on her shoes.

"Where you going?" York said to Mom. "We 'bout to eat. I know you gotta go to work, but can't you even eat with us?"

"Boy, calm down and mind your own business. Y'all set the table and warm up the food. I'm grown, don't ask me no questions," she said.

Yancy cracked open the door to find out where Mom was going; surprisingly, she went right over to Myrek's house.

My brothers and I stood in the doorway eavesdropping.

"I'm sorry things got a little out of control the other day, Mike," my mom said. "I have some food. It's New Year's Day and everybody deserves a good meal. Would you and the kids like to come over and eat with us?"

"Yvette, why would we want to do that? You're trying to tell my daughter what she's got to do with her baby."

"No, it's not gonna be none of that. I learned my lesson. Though I got strong views, I've just been praying about it. Some stuff I can't fix, like my ex-husband being in jail when I need him, you know? You just gotta learn how to roll with the punches and move on."

"See, why she gotta be talking about Dad to him?" York said as the three of us listened. "I don't want them coming over, eating our food. We got a refrigerator that's empty. We can have leftovers and grub for days. I sure hope he says no."

"Quit being selfish," I said to York.

"Yas just wants Myrek to come over here, Yancy," York said, getting under my skin like a bad rash.

"Yeah, she just wants Myrek to come over here," Yancy teased as he messed with my hair.

I wasn't even thinking like that. Myrek and I were cool with each other. We decided we had some feelings for each other, but we just want to be friends. We weren't trying to have nothing serious going on.

My two brothers had their issues. I still couldn't believe that Yancy hated being smart and detested being teased by his peers so much that he had started getting bad grades just so he wouldn't have to take accelerated classes. And finally he gets a girlfriend, Veida Hatchett. She was supposed to be my friend but had dropped me the first time I didn't like her being so fast with my brother.

And York wasn't any better, wanting to act like we had more than we did. He felt the need to dress in the fliest clothes so bad that he was willing to steal for them. Then he was arrested and had to perform community service.

Both of those things were stressing my mom out so bad. And then for her to find out that there's a chance that a part of my oldest brother could still be here on earth made her wrestle at night. I'm sure that's why she was unable to sleep at night; she was carrying so much on her. Yet she treated me like I was a kid and wouldn't talk to me like a friend who could take some of this stuff off of her. But I do feel bad that even though I didn't want to show her any resistance, I still gave her lip—more than she deserved.

"Let's get ready for our guests, y'all. Mom asked us to get the food ready. Let's just do it, okay?" I told them, trying to be a good daughter.

"You act like they're comin'," York said.

"Mom's over there asking them," Yancy said. "What else are they eating? They're just like us. Poor, trying to make it. They'll be over here for some food."

Sure enough, ten minutes later my mom came through the door with Mr. Mike, Myrek, and Jada. Myrek and I looked at each other with such awkwardness. We had been best friends since forever. But why did it feel different now? Maybe it was just because we were growing up. I thought he looked quite handsome in his new sweater that he must've gotten for Christmas—but I wasn't going to tell him that.

Teasing him, I said, "Make sure you don't eat up all the chicken legs. You know that's my favorite part."

Blushing and nodding, Myrek said, "For real, though, I'm glad your mom came over. My dad was fixing chicken noodle soup."

Jada said, "Hey, Yasmin."

I remembered the last time I had seen her, she was confessing that she had really hurt Jeff with some of the things she'd said to him. At that moment, I thought I could never forgive her. But then it was as if God pinched me. I had to move past this.

I said, "Can I talk to you for a second?"

"I'm really not up to it, Yasmin. I just can't deal with the stress. My dad and your mom have talked about this enough. I really want a good meal and then I'm going back to bed."

"I'm not gonna stress you out, but I do want to talk to you. Mom, we'll be right back," I said, heading to my bedroom. I wasn't taking *no* for an answer.

Sitting down on my bed, Jada said, "Okay. What? I was wrong and I'm sorry."

"Well, I'm sorry too for acting all high and mighty like I was judging you. I know you didn't mean for Jeff to go over the edge. He made that decision for himself. I guess I just wanted to let you know that I don't hold you responsible. That's all."

Looking surprised, Jada said, "Thanks, Yasmin." We hugged and then she and I headed to the kitchen.

Just then, I heard Mom and Myrek's dad laughing. For two people who weren't getting along a few days before, they were certainly acting chummy now.

"This ain't even gonna happen and go down like that," York said.

"What?" I asked.

"Myrek and Yancy are talking about getting the two of them together. That is not gonna happen as long as I'm here. No way."

I didn't know how I felt about that, even though my parents were divorced. With the divorce and my dad still being in jail, it didn't mean that he and my mom couldn't get back together when he got out. Mom had made a lot of sense when she said some stuff wasn't for us kids to get into. But whatever Myrek's dad was saying to her, it sure felt good to see her smile. The meal was a blessing to both of our families.

⁂

When I returned to school after the Christmas break, I thanked my English teacher, Miss Bennett, for coming by to help my family. I also went to my counselor's office to thank Mrs. Newman and to just talk.

"Mrs. Newman, I'm sorry that my mom didn't want to accept the help at first." Needing to vent, I went on, "You just don't even know. She is so strong. She does it her way, but it's like I don't even have any say over anything. Like she doesn't care at all what I think. Sometimes I get so tired of her acting like that. I don't have any hope that she's ever going to change and see me as the young woman I'm trying to be. Lately, York and Yancy have made bad choices. Then with my brother Jeff taking his own life—it's been really hard on her."

She touched my shoulder and said, "Listen, Yasmin, you just told me she's going through a lot. Don't lose hope in her. I believe your relationship will get better. You and your whole family will bounce back stronger from all that you had to deal with last year.

"Most people we minister to act as if they think they deserve stuff just being given to them. Your mom's not like that. She has integrity. She wants to provide for and take care of her kids. She may seem overprotective, but she's just a mama bear who's had some cubs wander a little too far away. And because your mom knows that you haven't, she just wants to do everything in her power to make sure you don't stray. There's love, honor, and strength in her."

I told Mrs. Newman about the drama between Myrek's family and mine and how my mom went over there with her Bible and then ended up really getting into it with Mr. Mike. Then a couple of days later Mom invited the family over to share the dinner that the church had blessed us with.

"Well, Yasmin, as you can see, just because a person is a Christian doesn't mean that they don't get angry and maybe say or do some things that they wish they hadn't. The important thing is that your mother extended herself to another family despite the conflict between you all. I'd say that your mom is really demonstrating the love of Christ—even in her own pain. And at the very least, thank God that she took the Bible with her!"

We had been through so much. And we weren't totally healed; the pain and the loss of Jeffery still hurt so badly. I had no idea what would happen with Jada, and I worried about York and Yancy going through their own tough times. I also had major concerns about my mom trying to keep our family on track. However, I knew I had to keep giving it all to Him.

Through it all, thankfully, God hadn't forgotten the Peace family. We were getting stronger each day.

Chapter 2

Remember
You Can

I can't believe you didn't see that fine guy on TV last night," Veida said, hardly letting me eat my lunch.

"What channel? What show? What was it about?" I asked.

"It was on channel 56, the new high school drama, *Georgia Sky*. That brother was so good looking. I would get with him in a minute."

"What's Georgia Sky?" I asked, knowing that another big reason why I didn't see it was because we don't have cable.

"It's a teen drama based on some books." Veida looked at me like I was clueless.

Next thing I knew, Perlicia plopped her tray down beside us. She had to have been eavesdropping. She was ready to jump into the A and B conversation that didn't C her anywhere in it.

Perlicia said, "Ohh, are y'all talking about that Dakari character on *Georgia Sky*? He is slamming; such a cutie."

Of course, I should have known Asia wasn't too far away. She always followed Perlicia. I wondered if she'd ever get a mind of her own. But Asia sat down too, and the three of them couldn't stop talking about how they wanted to be with this guy from TV.

I couldn't believe how graphic they were getting as they described the things they imagined doing with boys. Before our break for the holidays, Perlicia and Asia weren't really digging Veida. However, listening to them talk about their fantasies, you would think they were best friends.

"Okay, enough talk about sex already," I finally said, as Perlicia described something she'd seen on some adult channel she wasn't supposed to be watching.

I was just appalled. My mouth couldn't close. They wanted bigger chests to make the guys look at them more. Then they started naming guys in our eighth grade class and talking about how good or bad they thought their bodies were.

I silently prayed, *All right, Lord, I am right in the middle of a conversation that is repulsive to me. I can't even say these girls are supposed to be my friends. Our worlds are colliding. I have to sorta hang out with them. They're not even talking about what they did over the Christmas break. They're just talking about things Your Word says we can't do until marriage. Am I supposed to get my tray and move to another table? The only problem is, the girls over there seem to be focused on the same impure thoughts. Help me, Lord. Help me because I seem to be the only one who cares about pleasing You.*

"Quit being such a goody-goody," Veida said, seeing that I was very uncomfortable with their topic.

"Oh, I wish y'all could see this one guy from my old school that I used to date," Veida said as Perlicia and Asia inched closer, trying not to miss all the details she was about to spill.

"His name is Gabriel and last year it was like he was a seventh-grader trapped in a senior's body," Veida bragged.

"Oooohhhhh," Perlicia said. "I bet his chest was ripped. I can see him, girl! That fine Gabriel."

Veida said, "Yeah, and when he played basketball, you could really see his chest. All the girls were fighting over him."

I just looked at Veida like I couldn't believe she was saying this in front of me. After all, she and my brother Yancy had serious crushes on each other. Yet, if it wasn't some guy on TV she couldn't wait to go out to Hollywood and find, she was drooling over some boy she used to go to school with.

"What, Yasmin? Don't look at me like that. I'm sorry. I'm just a thirteen-year-old girl who's changing. I used to think about books and pleasing my parents, but now all I can think about is pleasing myself. Plus, my parents don't do everything right either. So why should I? You know what I'm sayin'?" Veida boasted, raising her hand for Perlicia to give her a high five.

Asia became a little distant. At first she seemed to be so into what was being said. I wasn't trying to figure out why she seemed to change. However, I was surprised by that.

"Okay, but what about pleasing God?" I asked as I stood up, unable to take any more of their drama.

Then they looked at me like I was crazy.

"Yeah," I said. "Pleasing God. He wants us to keep our minds pure, not all in a gutter somewhere. You know there are diseases out there, teen pregnancy, all kinds of craziness."

"I want to know more about that," Asia said, finally speaking up.

"As goody-two-shoes as you are, Yasmin, if you came down to

reality you'd know all that stuff people talk about doesn't even apply to us middle schoolers," Perlicia said. "We're not trying to go all the way. Just a little fun won't hurt nothing."

Veida nodded as if that comment made complete sense. I knew how girls became pregnant but a lot of girls didn't have correct information.

Asia started asking questions and saying what she'd heard about sex and pregnancy.

"Just because a boy touches you, what's the big deal . . . it's not sex," Veida said.

"Yeah, Veida, but that's what it will lead to. I know for sure that isn't a safe zone. So, Asia, don't believe their hype," I said.

Perlicia added, "As far as diseases go . . . they can cure everything nowadays anyway, even AIDS. Look at some of the big celebrities who have it. They're still around."

I hated that I didn't have the facts to dispute their claims, but none of that mattered anyway. If God wasn't happy with my actions and He told me I needed to wait, then that was all I needed to be concerned with. Why my classmates couldn't see it that way really bummed me out.

"Grow up, Yasmin," Veida said to me as I grabbed my tray and left them to their disgusting chat.

I tried to shove my lunch tray into the little hole for the ladies to clean it but it wouldn't go. I was getting so mad and then Mrs. Newman came over to me.

She said, "Okay, Yasmin, what's going on?"

"Ugh, it doesn't matter. I just feel like a first-grader trapped inside an eighth-grader's body."

"What do you mean? You're developing into a fine young lady.

You're just where you should be for your age. What's the matter?" she asked.

"All of the things girls my age are concerned with don't bother me at all, don't phase me at all, don't make me want to do it at all. I know they think I'm weird."

"So you've had a little lunchroom conversation with your girls, huh? You can't compare yourself to anybody else, and unfortunately, a lot of these girls around here are way too fast. You don't even know the half of it. They chase boys, skip school, and end up in a world of trouble. Unfortunately, most of them live to regret their bad decisions."

"I might be the only girl in school who doesn't care about all that. I just feel so out of place. Why does feeling the way God says I should stink so much?"

"We've got to do something about that around here because whenever a good girl thinks she is in the wrong, it's time for the adults to step up and add some clarity."

"Yeah, my friends know how they can get pregnant but they don't seem to understand or care about behavior that can lead them to sex. They think there are cures for all diseases, so it is no big deal to have sex."

"Yes, it's a very big deal. You have your cycle, then you go too far with a boy—and you *can* get pregnant. There are many sexually transmitted diseases, and everything *isn't* curable. I'm glad we talked about this, Yasmin. You are on the right track. Just because there is chaos around you, don't you go down the wrong path. Stay true to what you know is right. And even if you have to stand alone, keep standing."

I thought about what I knew in my heart to be true. It reminded me of the Scripture I'd learned in church: "Thy Word have I hid in my heart that I might not sin against thee." I didn't want to do anything that would displease God. God was truly in my world because He knew how much I really needed to hear what Mrs. Newman said.

⋙

When Yancy, York, Myrek, and I got off the bus later that day, Bone was sitting on his car. He called York to holla at him. But before York started over there, I told him that he needed to just keep it moving because Uncle John had already warned Bone about messing with us.

"Yasmin, please. You trippin', girl. I can talk to him if I want to. This ain't none of your business. You just try and keep up with yo' silly little friends and stay outta my business," York said.

"Man, Yasmin's right," Yancy said, "you got a hard head. You know Bone doesn't have anything good to say to you."

"Both of y'all need to mind yo' business. I don't answer to y'all," York said.

As we got closer to Bone and his homies, I noticed a gun in Bone's waistband. Everything in me was scared.

York stopped to talk to him and the rest of us stood close by. We might've been scared but we were all in this together.

York looked at us and said, "Y'all go on. I'll catch up with you. I gotta take care of something." Bone and his boys were looking us all up and down.

Then one of his boys said to Myrek, "What you lookin' at?"

Myrek just stared him down and then Yancy said, "Come on, y'all. Let's go."

Myrek couldn't stand Bone and hated the fact that his sister Jada used to kick it with him.

I didn't want to leave York there, but Yancy said that was a choice that York was making. He was going to have to deal with the consequences.

I was so mad. Yancy and Myrek were too. Myrek and I were walking very fast. I guess we were trying to beat our anguish away by hurrying.

"The two of y'all might as well run," Yancy said, trying to crack a joke.

Bone was big trouble and to see a gun up close like that was too personal to laugh about. We dodged a big bullet. It hurt me so to know that York still felt obligated to that thug.

When we got around the corner, I said to Yancy and Myrek, "Did y'all see that gun Bone had?"

Both of them said they'd seen it.

"You know they still ain't found them kids from a couple of summers ago. Everybody says Bone had something to do with it," I said.

"Somebody needs to take him down," Myrek said.

"I don't understand why the police can't throw away the key with that dude. He needs to be locked up," Yancy said.

Myrek said, "Naw, somebody needs to take him out! If only I could—"

"Myrek, don't talk like that. We're not like that. We're going to school. We're not going to drop out. We're going to get our education so we can get out of this hole we live in."

Out of my two brothers whom I shared our mom's stomach with, I had to admit Yancy wasn't the aggressive one. If there was a way that we could watch videos of right before we were born, York was probably the one kicking both of us. He just came out rougher and tougher.

"York always thinks he's a man and can handle everything for everyone. I'm sick of him tryin' to act all hard like Dad. Doesn't he understand he'll end up in jail too?" Yancy asked.

Then we saw York coming. Inside I was happy to see he was still in one piece. At least he was done dealing with Bone for now.

"Y'all looking like somebody stole your wallets!" York said.

Yancy and Myrek just looked at him and began walking ahead of us.

I had to be tough with York to let him know he needed to leave Bone alone.

"Why you actin' like you bad?" York asked me.

I started, "You don't owe him a thing. You don't have to try and defend our honor, thinking you got to work with a criminal to pay off some debt he said Jeff owed him, I don't even know if I believe that anymore."

"Yasmin, I believe it, so I'll take care of it the way I want to. I'm not going to let him push my sister around. I don't even want him messing with Yancy. Yancy ain't big and bad. It's not like he can handle himself with those guys. You just need to stay out of it and make sure he does too. I'm gonna handle what I got to handle. I wish I knew them books like y'all do, but that's just not my thing."

"It's because you don't try. You spend more time out here in the streets than you do in your books."

"Whatever, Yasmin."

"Just don't hang around them. You can get hurt. Please." I pleaded with him, trying not to come off too whiney.

"Just know that I got to do this. As far as Uncle John protectin'
us . . . he ain't here. I gotta do what I gotta do. He can't protect nobody and he's way down in Orlando. I got this. I just came to bring
my book bag home," he said as we approached the door. "I gotta roll
with Bone right now. If Ma asks where I am, you gotta cover for me
and make sure that Yancy keeps his punk mouth shut."

I didn't even get a chance to tell my brother that I wasn't going
to do it. I was so scared and didn't want anything to happen to York.
But as the wind started blowing in the cold January air, I felt like
God was saying, *Let Me be God and take care of York. You just go home
and take care of you.* As I entered our apartment, I thought, *Who
better to put my hope in?*

⋙

"Oh good, we got an assembly and I can sleep," my knuckle-
headed classmate Nelson said to me.

His partner just hit him in the chest and he started laughing.

"No, this will be inspiring. Someone is coming to talk to us
and get us ready for the writing exam—we gotta listen," I said.

"You listen," Nelson replied, mocking me.

There was an eighth-grade test mandated in the state of
Florida that we had to take; it would determine our writing apti-
tude. The school we attended didn't have the best test scores in the
county and a lot of us were nervous. The test wasn't going to keep
us from going on to high school, but it would determine our place-
ment in classes.

I didn't really know what I wanted to be in life, but I did know
some type of writing would be involved in whatever I chose. I
wanted to be successful in high school and go on to college. I

wanted to put my best foot forward on work that people would be judging me on. So, I was a little nervous. Yep, paying attention to the speaker was something I knew I had to do.

"All right, class," Miss Bennett said to everyone. "All the English classes are attending this assembly, and I don't want my class to be the one with students who don't listen. You give respect to this lady. Take in all the things she has to say because she can be doing so many other things with her time. Anybody who clowns, acts up, or embarrasses me will be given an in-school suspension."

Nelson asked, "Aww, come on, Miss Bennett. What if the lady is boring?"

"Boy, you definitely need to be listening to any pointers on how to write. I'm serious, you guys. No drama," she said.

"Yes, ma'am," we collectively said as a class.

When we got to the cafeteria there was a big poster of our speaker on the wall. Her name was *Stephanie Perry Moore*. She had all these books that she'd written. Most speakers we had would be sitting in a chair waiting to be announced, but she was at the door greeting all of us. She even told me that she loved my smile.

Then she said to Nelson, "Look at you, looking all fly today." He started smiling. I think she won him over.

The buzz going around was that the character from the TV show that Veida and Perlicia were so crazy about is based on her books.

"Guess you won't be talking now," I teased.

Nelson said, "Oh, shut up, Yasmin."

Miss Bennett's tough talk along with Mrs. Moore's greeting wasn't enough for everyone in the eighth-grade class to pay attention. Clear across the room Perlicia and Asia were laughing. Principal Caldwell got their attention and they hushed for a little bit, but I could tell that they were not into this at all.

Then our principal introduced our speaker. "I know quite a bit of planning has gone into getting Mrs. Stephanie Perry Moore here to talk to you guys. I've heard her before and you're in for a treat if you just sit back and listen. Like I tell you guys every time we have a speaker, they got theirs; listen to what they have to say so you can get yours.

"Some years ago, Mrs. Moore wrote the first African American Christian teen series entitled, *Payton Skky*. Since that time she has continued to be a trailblazer in young adult Christian fiction. She lives with her husband and three children and loves speaking to teens, telling them how they can be cool but still do it God's way. She came to us because a couple of our students have been in love with her books. So let's give it up right now for Mrs. Stephanie Perry Moore."

Hardly anybody clapped. Our students weren't the most polished bunch and we usually went with the flow. If one person booed, most would do that as well. Thankfully, no one did this time.

"How many of you guys have a dream and want to be successful? How many of you want to make a million dollars?" she asked, immediately taking the stage and not caring about how into it we were or weren't.

I could tell her goal was to get us into what she had to say. She had done it because everybody raised their hand.

"We all want to be somebody. Well, if you give me the next twenty minutes of your time, I promise I can help you achieve that dream or goal."

Perlicia and Asia were talking loudly again. Mrs. Moore walked over to where they were and placed her hand on Perlicia's shoulder.

"Everyone might not be into what I have to say, but that's okay. Let me just keep it real with you guys for a minute. Don't miss out on your blessing. If you want to take something from this talk, don't get caught up in what your friend is doing or saying to distract you. Stay focused for just a little while because at the end of the day, it's up to you to seize the moment.

"I appreciate your principal and your English teachers inviting me here today. However, today is not about me. So we are not going to talk about my books, shows, and all that. I'm standing before you because as an eighth-grader I had to take a test in Virginia that was similar to the one that you'll be taking. It may surprise you to know, but I took remedial English in the ninth grade. Yeah, I was one of those kids who laughed and joked with my friends, and cut up in class. I was real cool, popular, and had it going on . . . I thought I was all that."

A lot of us laughed. Some people stood saying, "Yeah that's me." It was obvious that we were into what she was saying.

"You see, while I was laughing, cutting up, and joking with my friends, they could flip the switch and I could not. When it came time to getting the work done, they understood the verbs, the prepositions, and everything else. And when I needed to take the test, I couldn't do it. My ninth-grade teacher at Matoaca High School, Mrs. Pulley, said to me, 'You can either take this seriously and set your life back on the right track—and get to learning where you want to go—or you can keep fooling around and flunk out.'"

I really hoped York was listening. I wanted him to know he could do it. He just needed to apply himself.

She continued, "You guys have a decision to make right now too. You can decide that you have to focus on getting what you need and doing what you need to do for yourself so that eventually you can achieve what you want to do. That next year I was in the creative writing class. That teacher aced me out of remedial English and I went on to bigger things. I never looked back when it came to the area of creative writing. Now I have over twenty-five books in print. But again, it's not about me today, it's about you. You've got a writing test coming up. You know all of the material. What's the first thing you do when there is a question posed to you?"

Veida raised her hand.

"Yes, ma'am," Mrs. Moore said, pointing to Veida.

"You understand what the question is asking, and then you start with an introductory topic sentence."

"Correct, and what are you supposed to do next?"

Yancy raised his hand and smiled, looking over at Veida as he said, "You write three sentences or more that support the main idea."

"Exactly, and before you wrap up that first paragraph, you need one more thing."

I raised my hand and said, "You need a closing sentence."

"Perfect, then there are three more paragraphs, which make up the body and contain information on all three points. After that what's next?"

Myrek raised his hand and said, "You have a closing paragraph that's basically the same as the first paragraph but you rework the sentences so you don't say the exact same thing."

"Exactly. Remember, guys, it's not about writing just to ace a test. I mean, yes, that's great and we want you to do the best you can, but this test is about setting you on the right high school path to get where you want to go in life. It took me seven years to get my first book published. During that time of personal setbacks, defeat, and inner turmoil, I remembered how I had to persevere in my ninth-grade year to make up for what I didn't get right when I took the eighth-grade writing test. You don't want to keep looking back to set your life right. Take advantage of it right now. You've got all the knowledge upstairs," she said as she pointed to her head.

"When it comes to taking that test, just remember you can."

Chapter 3

Enforcer
of Truth

I am so mad at my mom for signing this paper and making me be a part of LIGHT," Veida said as we waited on Miss Bennett and Mrs. Newman to work with us on an after-school program for girls. LIGHT is an acronym which stands for *Ladies Impacting Generations Here Today.*

"Well, if you didn't want to be here, why did you even give her the paper in the first place?" I asked.

"'Cause I was trying to stay after school for some other stuff. I wanted to spend time with your brother. I didn't realize that she was going to actually talk to Miss Bennett and tell her that she signed me up. So now I'm forced to sit in here," Veida pouted.

I wondered how my brother was planning to stay after school. *Oh yeah*, I thought. Without needing her to answer, I remembered he was tutoring some sixth-graders.

"So, Yancy wasn't going to tutor but hang out with you?" I asked.

She just looked at me and smiled probably thinking that was just a perfect idea for my brother to skip his responsibilities and hang out with her. She was so carefree that it killed me. The girl didn't know one thing about struggling. Her home life was so perfect. I wished just once she didn't have it so easy so she could appreciate something.

"I just want his arms all around me and our lips touching. Your brother is so romantic. If we could ever get some time alone—it's on!"

Then she shoved me in the arm. I don't know why Veida thought that I had changed my mind about getting physical with boys before we were married. She knew where I stood.

"Oh, just shut up, Yasmin. You're always so negative. Just because you don't have somebody to love. Well, you do, but you're scared of him and you're running from it, so you and Myrek pretend that there is nothing between you two. Fool whoever you want to, but don't rain on my sunshine."

"Do you two have to talk so loud? Y'all do more fussing than you do just communicating," Perlicia said from behind us.

I hadn't even looked back. I didn't know who all was going to sign up to be mentored; of course, wherever she was, Asia was there too. So I was excited and bummed all at the same time. I was excited that these three girls were in the room, because of all the eighth-grade girls, I knew they truly needed guidance. They were so far from trying to hear anything that would help that I couldn't imagine this making an impact. That was until the library door opened and we all sat up thinking our sponsors were coming in. However, Rhonda walked in. She was a girl who graduated from our school last year and was now a ninth-grader in high school.

She came over to us and said, "I'm here because of what's going on with me now. Miss Bennett and a lot of you guys already know anyway, if you have friends who go to my high school."

I didn't know what she was talking about. I remembered her being really popular. Actually, York thought she was all that. Her clothes always looked like they were made for someone four sizes smaller. I never passed judgment, thinking maybe she was like me and wearing all she had.

Rhonda continued, "My mom worked a lot and my body was growing fast. The boys gave me all kinds of attention and told me how cute I looked, and it went to my head. I was watching things on TV that I had no business looking at. The next thing I knew, I wanted to be with a guy. Then the next dude that came up to me and said something sweet . . . I was with him. I didn't stop with just one guy. I was just a little too fast all the way around. Naw, a lot fast."

"I just want one guy," Perlicia yelled out.

"Well, I'll tell you, I don't know if it's the first guy or the fourth guy that gave me AIDS," she said, shocking all of us. "All of them are being tested."

Nothing was funny at that moment. The looks on our faces were so horrific as if we had been watching a horror movie. It couldn't have gotten any worse.

"You guys are looking like you've never heard this. Everybody at my school has been talking about me and stuff. At first, I was so mad at the world and I blamed everybody else, but it was my fault and my decision to act grown. Not understanding what I was doing to myself really messed me up. I am here today to warn you guys not to walk in my shoes. I know we've all got to live our own lives, but take this from me, don't think this will never happen to you. I didn't think anything like this would ever happen to me either. So before you step out there—remember my story."

I raised my hand and sincerely asked, "Are you going to be all right?"

"Yeah, you're not dying or anything, are you?" Veida asked, as I hit her in the arm.

Rhonda said, "No, that's a fair question. I have a disease that is not going to go away, and it is not at the stage yet where it's extremely severe. However, I am going to be on medication all my life. And in a minute, it could elevate and take my life away. National studies show that one in four teenage girls between the ages of 14 and 19 have a sexually transmitted disease. Worse news— one in two African American teen girls have one."

Another girl who was so preppy and cute came up to Rhonda. She waved to us. We were all quiet for a second, waiting to see what's next.

Then the girl said, "Hi, I'm Jordan. I've got to be honest; to me my story makes me feel like I'm dying."

"You've got a disease too?" Perlicia asked her rudely.

"Naw, I just have a severely broken heart. I graduated from this school four years ago. I'm a senior now."

"Senior in the house! Senior in the house!" Perlicia responded, really not wanting anyone to talk her out of going too far with a boy.

"That's right," Jordan said, not letting Perlicia distract her. "Seriously though, I've come before y'all just to tell you that my dad warned me not to chase the boys. It's cool for boys to know you have it goin' on academically and socially. But I needed to demonstrate that I was valuable and not desperate for attention. All of this young love is something that doesn't really exist. It's just that when you meet a guy, you *think* you love him but you're just infatuated. I got a chance to be with the finest guy in high school, and I remember watching him roam the halls. He was all that. Then we got together."

"That sounds beautiful to me," Perlicia said.

"Well, the next day he acted like he didn't know me at all. He put my business out there; and honestly, I have never been the same since. He took a part of me that I can never get back. I just came by to let you guys know—all that glitters is not gold. Most of those boys are chumps and jokers. Y'all hear them talkin' about other girls. Why in the world would you think it's going to be different if you give it up?"

Jordan was so telling it straight. I wanted to shout like I was in church or something. Most dudes don't see girls as they should and treat them as princesses who are delicate.

Jordan was honest and said, "Nobody could tell me different. I never had a high school girl come by and talk to me. Maybe if one did, I would have listened. I don't know. So I just figured I would share with you what my dad told me that I didn't want to hear. He was right. Be smarter. After all, if the guy really likes you or even loves you, he'll wait. If he doesn't want to wait, you don't need him anyway, right?"

Then she headed to the door. I held my head low because all of the information we were getting was just so much. When I looked up, I was surprised to see Jada.

"Oh, my goodness! Isn't that your brother's old girlfriend?" Asia leaned forward and whispered in my ear. "Look at her stomach. She's pregnant."

Jada said, "I thought I could do this, y'all, but I can't! You can see why I came by to talk to you. The possibility of teen pregnancy is real."

She ran out crying. I went out in the hallway looking for her, but she had run out of the front door. All I could do was pray for her.

Miss Bennett pulled me back inside, "Listen girls, all three of their testimonies were extremely tough and painful for each one of those young ladies who came to talk to you. They all attended this school and they all had a lot of potential. They still do, but now they have other things to live with. As Jordan mentioned, be smarter."

"Some things we don't want you ladies to have to endure. Unfortunately, it seems like you guys are just thinking about one side of sex," Mrs. Newman spoke up. "Don't let a young man get you off course. You've got time—wait!!!"

No one said a word. We were all thinking about the three girls who had just stood before us. I couldn't speak for everybody, but I knew for sure that I was going to wait.

⋘◊⋙

When I got home later that day, my brothers were watching some dance show on TV where the girls practically had no clothes on. I was tired of boys thinking we were supposed to be paraded out for their enjoyment. So I went to the TV and turned it off.

"BET . . . when did we get cable anyway?" I yelled.

"Calm down. Besides, don't worry. I got the hookup. Why you turning off the TV? You ain't payin' for it," York said as he walked over and turned the power back on.

"You always into something illegal. Some kind of quick fix," I charged York. "Yancy, I thought you hated that but you're going along with this, sitting there and enjoying that TV show, acting like it's okay."

"We're just checking out the hotties," Yancy said with a mischievous grin on his face.

"Please, you gon' get us in trouble with this bootleg cable stuff," I said, rolling my eyes at both of them. "Don't you think that Ma will see it one day when she turns on the TV?"

"Oh shut up, Yasmin," York said, shooing me out of the way. "You know as tired as Ma is when she gets home from work, the last thing she's lookin' at is TV. Quit being such a goody-goody. If you don't want to watch it, go to your room. Go do some homework or somethin'."

York definitely had a point about that. Mom almost never watched TV. Still, it was amazing to me that he was willing to take the chance and get caught. Unfortunately, that's how some people are. Big Mama said some people take a risk knowing that there are consequences. She said they would enjoy sin for a season. York was definitely one of those people.

Then we heard keys jingling at the front door. The two of them couldn't scramble fast enough to turn the TV off. I so wanted to blab to Mom.

As soon as she stepped inside with a box of fried chicken, she said, "What in the world is all that fussin' going on? I can't even come in the house and surprise my children with a nice meal without getting frustrated because y'all goin' off on each other. I'm sick and tired of this, you guys. You say you're old enough, but I leave you here only to find out that you can't get along."

All three of us stood to attention like she was a captain in the army and we were under her command. I certainly knew I was sick and tired of getting into trouble for what they were doing. I needed to clear my name.

Quickly, I said, "Ma, I ain't do nothing. It was them."

"I know I heard a TV in here and I ain't never known any of you to watch the news. That's all that's on at this hour with the three channels we got, so what were you watching? And how were you watching it? Somebody bought some DVDs?"

Yancy and York looked at each other. They were such clowns they could have been in somebody's circus. I knew they would try to sweet-talk her to wiggle out of trouble. Sure enough, they did.

"Let me help you with that food you're carrying," York said, trying to change the subject.

"Yeah, Ma, let me get your coat," Yancy said, walking over to her.

The next thing I knew she was relaxing, while one of them was stroking her feet. They were such con artists. I rolled my eyes from here to Texas.

"Yas, honey, York and Yancy, I need to talk to all three of you guys."

"What's going on, Ma? Why you at home this time of day anyway?" I asked.

"I tried to tell you all that I could come home at anytime. I said y'all need to be doing the right thing because you never know when I'm going to show up. You're so hardheaded, though. You've gotta do it your way. Beware—if you do wrong, I'm goin' to catch you."

"We wasn't doin' nothin' wrong, Ma," York said, looking at Yancy like he'd better not say anything.

They knew not to look at me because I would sing like a canary if I wanted to. They never had my back on nothing and I knew their minds didn't need to be corrupted by those horrible videos. As much as I wanted her to check them and let them get in trouble, I decided not to say anything. So I just sat down and listened to her.

"I got offered a job today. A real job, something that can give me benefits and retirement." She lifted her hands in the air celebrating herself.

"What? For real, Ma?" Yancy said in a skeptical tone. "How did you get something like that?"

I could tell he wished he could take back those words he said, not wanting to hurt her feelings. For years she had tried to get a better job, and they always told her that she didn't qualify. She'd come home and talk about her many disappointments with us. We just figured without an education there was no such thing as something stable. Anyway, a real career for her—all I could think is, *God is good!*

"I'm gonna be trained as a medical technician," she smiled.

"Ma, that sounds like good money," York said.

"Yes, it is. I feel that having had four babies and raising y'all up, I know a lot about sickness. I've got a lot of home remedies in me, but now I can get some training and really be able to provide for you guys in a few years. I won't be paid the good money instantly because I have to get fully trained. But it's supposed to come. I've got to go to Miami for some schooling, but I'm just not sure if I can take the job."

"What you mean, you're not sure?" York stood up and said.

"Well, son, I don't want to leave y'all. Every time I start thinking I can, y'all are fussin' about somethin'. Imagine if I'm gone for a week. You guys will kill each other," she uttered as she quickly covered her mouth.

No one said anything at that moment. We knew our mom was making a joke, but for some reason we all thought of Jeff. Even she realized that her words didn't come out right. Wasn't nothing funny about us killing ourselves or each other.

"Kids," she said, with open arms, as we all began embracing her. "What Jeff did was horrible and it affects us all, but we gotta learn how to move on and live a little. We've gotta be able to make jokes and live like regular people. We can't hold this thing so close to the vest, though the whole ordeal was horrible and I see you guys are still grieving. We may never totally understand why Jeff took his own life but now we have to trust God for each of our own lives. When we had our family counseling sessions at the church, remember we talked about lettin' go of the past and reachin' forward to what God has for us as a family?"

We all nodded. The counseling sessions had helped us cope even though Pastor Newman said we still would have days when we'd feel down.

Mom said, "I can't leave you all alone right now. I can't go for the training," she said, hitting the table.

"Why don't you have someone come and stay with us?" I said.

"I already called Big Mama. She's not able to come up here because she still has to keep your cousins after school." My cousins Alyssa and Kyle were Mom's sister, Yolonda's kids.

"Then what about Uncle John?" Yancy said excitedly.

"Whatever," York responded with the air totally out of the balloon. "I don't want him over here. He don't need to come and babysit me. Naw, that's not gonna work!"

Yancy went over to York and said, "If Uncle John is able to come up here and help us out, then who cares what you think? You are so selfish. This could stop Ma from getting her opportunity. How could you not support that?"

"All right, Ma," York sat down and didn't act mad. Surprisingly, he went over to her. "I ain't no dream killer."

"Son, I really appreciate you. Y'all know I wouldn't bring nobody here who I didn't trust to take care of y'all," she said.

York said, "I'm all right, Ma. It's cool. If he can come, then I'm cool."

She responded, "You'll have to respect him though, son."

"He'll have to respect me," York said.

"Boy, be quiet," Mom said.

"Ma, we'll be fine. You've got to go and do this for you. Nothing is going to go wrong with us." I hugged her.

She smiled and gave me a big kiss. I could tell she wanted this chance. We were with her.

"Girl, I hope you're right because, if I come back and your uncle tells me that he had any problems, I'm going to beat all of y'all's behinds."

The three of us just laughed.

"Oh, you think I'm playing, huh?"

"We're proud of you, Ma," Yancy said.

"Truth is, I wouldn't want no big time job if it wasn't for y'all. I'm gonna get my babies what they need. I don't want y'all to have to hustle and do nothin' extra. I'm gonna do my part. Y'all three just make sure you do yours."

"We will, Ma. Well, I promise. I can't speak for your crazy sons," I said as I hit both my brothers and ran.

"I know you all had better be good," she said. "Uncle John don't play."

⧫

"Look man, I don't need you comin' up in my spot embarrassin' me in front of my crew and stuff," York said, the very next week as he went off on Uncle John. "You ain't in charge of me. I told Ma I'm grown. I don't need no babysitter in the first place. So, thank you, but no thanks. You can go on back to Orlando as far as I'm concerned. I got this. Now I look like a punk in front of my boys."

"York, you need to quit," I said, shaking my head.

"Yasmin, mind your business, girl!" York said.

"Boy, please," My uncle said, lightly whacking my brother upside his head. "You ain't nowhere near grown. You don't know what kind of trouble you're getting yourself into," Uncle John said boldly as he ushered York back toward our apartment with Bone looking on.

"You down there in another city. You don't know how hard it is for us up here," York shot back.

Uncle John said, "I know you miss your daddy."

"That's right and you *ain't* my daddy."

"Naw, but I promised him I'd hold it down. And since I don't have my own kids, you guys are like my—"

"Look," York interrupted, "I ain't tryin' to hear all that."

I hated that York was so disrespectful. My uncle had taken off a week from driving his truck, and being with our sweet Aunt Lucinda, to come and be here for us. I couldn't even enjoy having the bed to myself, because there was so much tension in the house.

When we got back to our apartment, York went to his room

and slammed the door. I said to my uncle, "I'm sorry he's so rude. I don't know what's gotten into my brother."

"He's a hothead like your dad. I grew up with it. I'm used to it. I'm just trying to get him to calm down though, before he gets himself into trouble he can't get himself out of. For some reason he thinks that I don't care about him and that's not true at all."

"Let me go and talk to him," I said to my uncle, who seemed completely frustrated.

I needed to talk some sense into York. He kept on hanging with Bone. It was bad enough that Bone dealt drugs, robbed stores, and stole cars. But he had also been questioned in a murder investigation and though there was never enough information to put him in jail, our whole community suspected he was guilty. Why York couldn't see it baffled me.

"Knock, knock. Can I come in?" I said as I walked into his room without an invitation.

York said, "Yasmin, don't start!"

"I'm just saying, York, all that stuff you are into with Bone is illegal."

"You don't even know what we do."

"York, look at me. Look at me and tell me the stuff he is into is legit!" My brother couldn't look me in my eyes.

"Uncle John just don't know what he's doin' flexin' his muscles around Bone. I know I don't owe him my life, but I do owe a debt."

"Like I said before, York, you don't owe him nothing. That's what he said Jeff owed him. You know he's probably lyin'. How can we really believe that he was affiliated with Bone in the first place?"

"It's deeper than all of that now, anyway. If you, Yancy, Myrek, or Uncle John come in and pull me away, I'll owe more because of the disrespect. Plus, he's throwing a couple of dollars my way . . . and the cable hook up.

"Bone gives me protection. It's like a family that's really there for me. He feels the stuff that I need. No school books and no minimum wage job can take care of me now," York said, pulling out twenty-dollar bills and flinging them on the bed.

"Yeah," I told him. "It's about stealing from the poor and selling your soul to the devil."

"God don't want me."

"I can't believe you would say that," I said in disgust as I opened up the door only to find my uncle standing right there.

"What you doing eavesdropping on our conversation?" York sounded all mad when he saw him.

"I wasn't, but I have a right to. Where's Yancy?"

York laughed. "He's probably at school studyin' or somethin'."

Uncle John said, "He should be home by now."

York looked at me and I looked back at him. We both couldn't even look at our uncle. Yancy would never have been tutoring this long. He was with Veida for sure.

"Okay, what is it that y'all are not saying?" Uncle John asked.

All of a sudden the front door opened and Yancy walked in. "I'm home. I'm home. The master of love is home."

"Boy, where have you been?" Uncle John went up to the front of the apartment and asked.

"I've been . . . I've been tutoring," Yancy said, stumbling over his words.

"Don't lie to me, boy," Uncle John said.

"It ain't like you gon' do nothin' to him no way. You just like embarrassin' me and keeping me straight, but Yancy's little goody-two-shoes self is out there trying to do grown man things too."

"What is he talking about, Yancy?"

"Uncle John, I got a girl," Yancy said, trying to play it off like his lying was no big deal.

"What you mean, you got a girl? You told me you were going to be at school. You tryin' to get your groove on. Boy you wouldn't even know what to do with all of that. How you gon' play me? I trusted you."

"I just didn't want you worrying," Yancy said, clearly upset that Uncle John was disappointed with him.

"Boys, sit down. Now!" he shouted in a tone I'd never heard before. "Somewhere over the last twenty-four hours, you guys got it twisted. I'm in charge. That means you don't go to the bathroom unless I know about it. I don't care if you hate my guts or if you think you love me so much that because of our bond, I will be fooled by the lies you tell . . . don't try me. I know every kid needs a father around. So many things can happen to them when you don't have that strong influence in your lives every day.

"But you don't have to have a father around all of the time to have integrity and wits about yourself. If you think at thirteen that you know it all, that idiotic point of view will land you in jail or being somebody's daddy at too early an age. And as long as I am here, I'm going to give you what I think you need. I'm going to stay on you. You're going to do it my way. If you want respect from me, you have to be honest about what's going on. I am an Enforcer of Truth!"

Chapter 4

Over
the Hurt

York, Yancy, Yasmin, get yourselves up right now and get in here!" my uncle hollered out just as we were going to bed. The three of us flew to the front of our apartment. He sounded very aggravated. His voice was so authoritative. We hadn't heard an adult male's voice in our house in so long that it commanded all of our attention and instantly we were there.

Grudgingly, York said, "What? I'm tired."

"Yeah, Unc', couldn't this have waited until tomorrow?" Yancy asked.

Our uncle didn't respond to the whining. I knew whatever had him mad, I didn't to it. He motioned for us to follow him to the kitchen. Then he flipped on the light in the kitchen, and I lost it.

In the midst of our surprise reaction, Uncle John asked, "Why are y'all so nasty? Roaches are everywhere!"

The little bugs started moving fast when the light came on. They were everywhere in varying sizes and colors. It was absolutely disgusting. For real, we weren't nearly that dirty.

"Ohh, they're on the countertops!" I said.

When York moved the bread, even more came crawling out. I couldn't hold back the uneasiness I felt. I started scratching everywhere.

"I see why you called us," Yancy said. "But we didn't do this."

"Listen guys, roaches just don't show up. There's something about your habits. Something about the way y'all are living that's making them come out like this."

"All our stuff from the refrigerator is closed up. Ma has been on us about that," Yancy said as I nodded in agreement.

Then we heard noise coming from next door. It wasn't on Myrek's side, the problem existed on the side closest to our kitchen. Miss Sandra was shouting.

"It might not even be y'all at all," Uncle John said. "This may be coming from someone else's mess. Your mom told me about that lady next door and how she can't take care of her children. Maybe she can't clean up either," Uncle John said.

Let's go over there and talk to her right now," York said as he opened the door.

When we got to Miss Sandra's apartment door, Uncle John said to York, "Boy, get back. I can handle this," as he knocked lightly on the door.

"She gets some stuff from Bone. You might need to knock a little harder." York said behind my uncle's back.

Uncle John said, "Boy, didn't I tell you to get back?"

"I'm just sayin'..." York said with a sharp tone.

I stepped to the door and offered, "Maybe hearing from me, she'll open up the door. Miss Sandra, it's me, Yasmin."

Quickly, she came to the door. Holding her two-year-old son, Dante, she asked, "Y'all got any bug spray?"

As the four of us walked into her place, we were grossed out even more. We thought our place was bad. She had triple the roaches all over the place. She couldn't blame anybody else for her mess because she lived in the end unit. Her five-year-old daughter, Randi, grabbed my hand. Sometimes I babysat for her and Dante.

"Help me, Yasmin! The bugs are getting me! They're everywhere!" she exclaimed.

"Oh hush, girl, it ain't that bad," Miss Sandra said to her frightened young daughter.

"Ooh, who are you?" she asked as she checked out my uncle. "I ain't known Yvette had a new man."

"He's our uncle," we said to her in unison, obviously thinking alike.

"Yeah, I'm their uncle. My name is John."

There were all kinds of food out on her countertops. The bugs were having a good time crawling all over the food. I could've puked.

"I gotta cover up this stuff," Miss Sandra said.

"No, you gotta throw this stuff out," my uncle responded. "You gotta do something to get these roaches out of here. They've made their way over to our apartment now!"

"Yeah, some of the tile and stuff is comin' down from the wall. See?" she said, as she went over to a corner and pointed. Through the wall, we could see from her kitchen into ours.

"Oh, uh huh!" my uncle sighed. "The management has to do something about all this quick."

Miss Sandra said, "If I have to wait on them, I don't know

when that'll be. That's why I need y'all to help me get rid of them."

Uncle John responded to her plea. "I wish my wife and I were blessed with children to take care of. Even so, I'm thankful that I can take care of these three rugrats," he said with a smile. Then with a stern voice, he continued, "But you got young babies. You gotta wanna do better for yourself," he told her, looking around the filthy place with disgust.

She started crying. "You just don't know how hard it is tryin' to make it. I ain't got no husband."

"I ain't got?" York said over in my ear. Even he knew that was bad English.

"Hush, boy!" I said to him wishing he wouldn't worry about someone speaking correct English at a time like this.

"I don't know what to do with this baby," Yancy said referring to Dante, whom he was trying to calm down from crying.

"Nobody helps me. I tried to get a job, and daycare is too high. My kids get sick and then I miss work. I got two different baby daddies and neither one of them show up for nothing. I'm doin' the best I can. Besides, I grew up with roaches. They ain't never killed me. Y'all lookin' at me like I'm giving my kids the plague or something."

"Nobody's trying to look down on you," Uncle John went on. "I'm just saying that it's a problem now that they're invading my sister-in-law's place. My mother was a single mom too. She tried to do the best she could. It was hard. I understand and tomorrow we're gonna try to help you out."

Both York and Yancy made grumbling and grunting noises in protest. Uncle John was certainly running our household because he didn't care if they disapproved. He made it clear that after school we were going to help clean up her place and ours.

The next day that's exactly what we did. The hole that was in the wall was gone. I guess while we were at school, Uncle John worked with the management to get it fixed. An exterminator sprayed down the place and because Miss Sandra had already spent her food stamps for the month, Uncle John bought groceries for her and us too. Even York had to admit he was an all-around good man.

He was good with Miss Sandra's kids too. I really felt bad that he and my aunt had been trying for a couple of years to have a baby and couldn't. It would have been easy for him to be bitter and not help someone else. Thankfully, he put aside all of his past pain and reached out to make a difference. What a great role model he was for us.

⋘◈⋙

The week had flown by since my uncle had come and he had gotten us in line—big-time. Yancy wasn't making up any more stories about tutoring appointments that didn't exist. In fact, he was coming home after school and tutoring York. I wouldn't have believed it if I hadn't seen it for five straight days. But my brothers were actually in a rhythm. They were learning how to appreciate each other's strength. York needed help and Yancy wanted to feel needed. Uncle John helped them tear down the wall that was between them and build back up the bond that being a family was all about.

Miss Sandra had even made a home cooked meal from the groceries my uncle bought her a couple of days before and offered us some. Even though we turned down the offer, her gesture was really sweet.

Mom was coming home the next day and we had the place spotless. We cleaned with such detail that we even scrubbed the bathroom tile with toothbrushes. It was immaculate. Uncle John bought new bedspreads for my brothers' room and removed Jeff's bed and all of his clothes. We told Uncle John that Mom wanted to clean out Jeff's things but that she hadn't gotten around to it. He decided to do it so that when Mom returned, she wouldn't have to deal with the painful memories.

With things being so good, something was still nagging me and I couldn't sleep. When I flipped on the light in the kitchen to get some water, I was very glad that there wasn't a roach in sight. As hard as I was trying to be quiet and not disturb my uncle, I was sorry that I had awakened him.

"Yas, is that you? Girl, what's going on? You're supposed to be asleep."

"I'm sorry. I didn't mean to wake you," I responded.

"I know you don't have school tomorrow, but it's twelve-thirty in the morning. You all right? You know we can talk anytime."

I just dropped my head and sat at the kitchen table. "I don't know where to begin. Something's wrong with me and I can't quite put my finger on it."

"Aww, it's that you're gonna miss me, huh?" he said, as he lightly gave me a box hit in the arm.

"Yeah, Uncle John, I'll miss you. Not that I'm not excited about my mom coming back or anything like that. I miss her so much. I can't wait to give her a big hug and hear all about her training and stuff. Yeah, I guess I am gonna miss you. But you'll come back and visit, right?"

"Yeah, you know I'm coming back; so that's not it, is it?" he asked.

"I don't know. I just need some water. I'll be fine."

"Talk to me, girl. I hadn't been the best uncle, being so far away. I've been so focused on my own life and busy takin' care of my wife and job that I just hadn't been around for my own brother's kids. This week here with you guys has been extra special. Y'all need me."

"Maybe that's the problem, Uncle John. Maybe it's not you that I'm really gonna miss. Maybe having you around has shown me how much I miss my dad."

"I don't understand. He's been gone for awhile."

"Yeah, but having a male around the house, I mean, even Jeff wasn't like a dad to us. He thought he was, but he wasn't." We both laughed. "But having you here, taking care of us, keeping us straight, getting on York and Yancy is stuff me and Mom really can't do anymore. It just meant a lot. I mean, you even helped Miss Sandra next door. I don't know. If I had my own dad here . . . "

As sorrow gripped my heart, I couldn't finish the sentence. Tears just fell. Built up pain, frustration, and hate that I didn't even know I still had came rushing from inside of me to the outside. I didn't want any sympathy from him. I didn't want his hugs.

I blurted, "I thought I didn't need a dad. I thought that it didn't matter that he wasn't here with me on a daily basis. And I've gotten over the fact that my brothers were mad that he . . . I mean, York wants him here but Yancy and Jeff, they just . . . they just were through with it, you know? And I'm just so mad at my dad right now. He should be here!"

"I know. I understand how you're feeling. It's okay to express that."

"It's not okay. He's locked up!" I said as tears continued to fall. "You got us on track in just a week. If Dad was here every day, no telling where we'd be with his guidance. Even with Ma and him being divorced, if he weren't in jail, I know he'd be helping. People often say that it's better if you're in a two-parent household. I always thought that was so stupid because strong moms can do it alone. But really they can't."

He looked down, took a deep breath, and then said, "Well, they can because they have to. They don't have a choice. Your mom is doing an excellent job with you three."

"Uncle John, my brother is gone. There is not a day that goes by that one of us doesn't wish that he was still here.

"What if Dad would have been here? If Jeff didn't feel like he had to be the man taking on so much, maybe he wouldn't have been so depressed."

"That may be true, Yasmin. But we don't know that. We have to make sure that we don't place blame and become bitter. You've got one of the biggest hearts I know. I've seen you around here praying before every meal and having a conversation with God before you go to bed. You've got to trust God with this. I'm praying your dad gets out soon. I know he wants to make up for a lot of his mistakes."

"Like Ma's gonna let him come back in this house."

"Well, that's up to her. Either way he can help your mom out some, especially if you guys are open to it."

What my uncle said made a lot of sense. Maybe Dad could still add value to my life. I knew that he loved us. Maybe if I focused on that love, it would help me get over some of this excruciating turmoil.

⇜❧⇝

"Ma, you're home!" we screamed the next morning as the four of us sat eating cereal when she opened up the door.

"York, look at you, boy. You got a few more muscles on you. Oh my goodness! And Yancy, you look like you're taller. Yasmin, how pretty you are, girl. These men didn't drive you crazy did they?"

"No, it's been a good nine days, Mom. We missed you, though," I said, squeezing her extra tight.

"So what's been going on here since I've been gone? I know y'all gotta catch me up on all sorts of stuff."

My brothers dashed outside to get Mom's bags. "Okay, my sons are rushin' to be helpful and I don't even gotta ask them. John, what have you done? And it really looks good in here. I thought I was gonna have to come home and make them clean up on their Saturday. I'm impressed."

"Thanks, and you didn't even think I could do the job, huh?" he said to her.

"All right, you're right. I had my doubts. Words taken back. Thank you. It was a great week of training. I get paid in a couple of weeks and I'm on the road to getting my babies a better life. Oh, Yasmin! I love you, girl," Mom said extremely nice.

I wanted to say, *Okay what have you done with my mom?* Instead, I just enjoyed the love.

"Yas, tell me you guys were good for your uncle."

"Oh, they were good," Uncle John said before I could get a word in.

"Ma, Uncle John cleaned out Jeff's things for us and he even helped Miss Sandra with bugs that had infested her apartment. Those critters had started coming over here. He bought groceries for her and her kids and everything," I said.

"Wow! I appreciate that more than you know, John. Helping us and even my neighbor who's struggling, God is gonna bless you in a major way. I can't wait to see it!" she said excitedly.

"Yvette, I'm just glad that I could help. I'm looking forward to seeing what God is gonna do in all of our lives," Uncle John said.

"Well, I got some stuff for you guys," she said.

As she and I went and peeked out the door, Mom said, "Boys, what's takin' y'all so long?"

They were outside talking to Jada and Myrek. Mom didn't yell out like usual. She smiled at seeing them.

Uncle John said goodbye to Mom and I and told us that he'd catch Yancy and York outside.

"I do need to talk to her," my mom said, looking at Jada. She called to Jada to come inside, "Can I speak to you for a second, sweetie?"

"Yeah . . . yes, ma'am," Jada said reluctantly.

Just then, Mr. Mike came to the doorway, and he and Jada headed for our apartment.

"I just wanted to apologize for being so forceful with you. Telling you that you couldn't get rid of this baby and all that stuff was wrong. The more I think and pray about it and ask God for direction, I realize that it's your body and your choice. Whatever decision you make, I want you to know that I care about you. Though that's my grandbaby, and I know God is the giver of life, I had no right being so overpowering."

"Well, that's certainly the truth!" Mr. Mike interjected.

"Well, that's why I'm apologizing to the girl now, if you don't mind," Mom said to him.

Mr. Mike touched my mom's arm and said, "No, I'm just playing. I appreciate you taking time to talk with her like that. She didn't want to let you down, of all people, in this decision."

"I didn't want to let God down either," Jada said. "I'm gonna have this baby. I'm too far along to do anything other than that. However, the decision to keep the baby—I'm just not sure."

"And I shouldn't have tried to force you," my mom said hugging Jada.

"You just don't know, Mrs. Peace, what it does for me to hear you say this. I have been praying and wondering what your son would want me to do. And, forgive me, if I don't keep this baby. I just believe Jeff would want me to do what's best for me and the baby. Maybe I'm not being the best parent right now."

We were having a serious meeting. But it wasn't hostile like the previous heated discussion at the beginning of the year. People were hearing each other and cared about one another's needs. It wasn't an *"I"* mentality anymore. God was truly answering prayers.

Jada and Jeff had made a mistake. But did Jada have to be a parent for the rest of her life when there were great people who were ready and willing and wanted to care for a child? As bad as my mom wanted to raise the baby, she couldn't do it. She was struggling to take care of the three of us. Myrek's dad was doing the same for his family.

Mr. Mike said, "Listen, we've been looking at a couple of agencies that would allow her to still be in contact with the baby."

"But, Dad, I'm not saying that I'm giving the baby up."

"I know, baby, I know. I do want you to be a part of this whole thing though, Yvette. If you don't mind."

"For my grandbaby, I'm here however you need me. If that's

what you feel like you gotta do, Jada, I'm gonna support you in that."

"Thank you," Jada exclaimed, throwing her arms up in the air.

Again, this was all so weird. I couldn't believe that my mom was being so cool about this. With Mom knowing that a part of Jeff was inside of Jada, and that she wouldn't have a continual say in the baby's life if Jada gave the baby up for adoption—yet she stayed cool with that—I was really amazed. My mom and Jada hugged again, and this time it lasted about two minutes. Mr. Mike became very emotional as he watched them.

He said, "Yeah, she's not trying to hurt nobody, but my daughter ain't ready to be a mom yet either. This is just hard."

"I know," Mom said as she and Jada's embrace ended. "We're gonna have to figure this out together. A baby is coming into the world. This is a happy occasion. We gotta rejoice. Again, I apologize. I was closed-minded about the situation at first, but I'm past all that. Now, I'm thankfully over the hurt."

Chapter 5

Easier to Forget

"Ma, we got letters from Dad!" York said more excited than I'd heard him in weeks.

The letters had been sitting on the table all day. York was just the one not home. Now that Uncle John wasn't around, York was back to his old ways of hanging out with Bone and his thug crew. Mom was working so much and he had no accountability. Forget what I tried to tell him and he wouldn't listen to Yancy either. He was just stepping back into trouble. Maybe Dad's letter could turn him around—but I doubted it.

"So, y'all not gonna open 'em?" York asked. "Y'all just got them sitting here. Ma, here's yours," York said as he picked it up and handed it to her.

"Yasmin, he even drew a heart on yours," Mom said, rolling her eyes playfully.

"Open it," my brother said as he tossed it across the room to me.

Then York hollered, "Yancy, come out and get Dad's letter."

"I'm studying. I don't wanna read that," my brother yelled from the bedroom.

"Daddy ain't sent us letters in all the time he's been in jail. Now finally, he's probably pouring his heart out, and y'all won't even open up the letters. That's trifling," York said, opening up the front door and slamming it behind him.

"I just don't understand your brother. Just because he's all excited about your father writing a word or two down on paper and the rest of us aren't, he thinks we're such bad people. I write notes to you all almost every day."

"What, Ma?" I said laughing.

She went on, "Take out the trash. Don't forget to do your homework. Be good in school. . . . And I also say what at the end of every note that I leave y'all?"

"I love you," I answered.

"Exactly, and I don't see y'all going crazy about my stuff."

I wanted to tell her it wasn't a competition, and at least it was a good thing that York loved Dad. If she knew all the stuff her tough son was into, she'd want him to be talking to somebody in jail. Maybe then he wouldn't end up there by making similar bad choices. But I couldn't go there. I couldn't divulge any of my brother's secrets, even though I felt like I was doing him more harm than good by keeping my mouth shut. It was all just a mess.

I went to the back of the apartment and peeped in the room at Yancy. He wasn't even studying. He was reading a book. There was nothing wrong with reading a book, but he said that he was too busy to come out and get Dad's letter.

"So, why don't you wanna see what he's got to say?" I asked.

"It's just better for me if I don't even open the thing. Why would I want to read his stupid promises? He's not doing anything for me. He's not doing anything for any of us, York included. If Dad were any kind of a father, he'd be here helping us. You know what I'm saying, Yas?"

"Yeah, I feel you, but we can't be mad that York really loves Dad. Maybe we should just open them up and see what he has to say," I suggested.

"Look, Yas," he stood up and came to the doorway where I was standing, "if that's what you want to do, then you should do it. I'm a guy. I got real issues with Dad. I know girls need a father figure and all that stuff, and Uncle John told me a little bit about . . ."

"Uncle John told you what I said?"

"I mean, it wasn't any confidential stuff. He just said you miss our father. He actually was telling me because he wanted me to not be so against Dad ever coming back here—which I still am."

I said, "Well, I'm not saying that I think Dad needs to be here or not. I mean, I just don't know. It's neither of our decisions to make anyway. Besides, I think Ma and Mr. Mike might get together."

"You know York and I are not for that, especially York," Yancy continued.

"But again, it's not y'all's decision to make," I said.

"Yeah, but you don't need to push that. Ugh, he lives right next door to us." Yancy went on, "Ma ain't been out in years. She's been privately thinking, hoping, and wishing that Dad was gonna come back and rescue her. Then we'd all be some big, happy family again. That certainly is not the way it is and I don't care what he says in any letter. He can't change the fact that he's locked up and not here for us when we need him. I don't care what he has to say. I don't want to hear it."

As I walked out of the room, Yancy shut the door. What more could I say?

"Yasmin," Mom called.

"Yes, ma'am?"

"You gon' open up your letter, honey?"

"I don't know. Did you open up yours, Ma? " I asked walking into the kitchen.

"Yes, I did open mine and your dad just encouraged me to keep doin' a good job with you guys. He said that he looks forward to gettin' out so he can be a good dad to you all. Sweetheart, I can see you're toiling with this whole thing. You've been pacing around here for hours before York even came home and got all excited. Your relationship with your father is yours alone. I know he loves you. People ain't perfect; they make mistakes. And parents sometimes make the worst decisions, but just like God gives us grace, we gotta do the same for others."

"Ma, I'm glad you opened the letter and that it said good things. But I was just wondering—do you like Mr. Mike?"

She just started smiling.

"I don't know who I like and it's none of your business. Open your letter. Bye, girl, you got a room all to yourself."

I went and sat on the bed and opened up the letter. I was amazed as I stared at the page filled with the three words: *I love you.*

The last paragraph read, *"I know I've hurt you, baby. I've had so much time to sit and think and wish I could make it different, but I pray for you daily and I know in my heart that God's got you. Soon, I'm hoping for the opportunity where I can be your dad again and we can erase some of the pain I've caused you. Again, much love, Your Daddy."*

I just took the letter and held it tightly to my chest. *He loves me*, I thought. Boy was that great to know.

⤞⚬⤝

"So, um . . . you wanna go to the dance with me?" Myrek asked as we walked to class. It was the week of Valentine's Day.

I had to admit he really looked cute with his perfect smile, pressed jeans, and his glowing complexion. Besides, I wasn't crazy. I saw the girls walking down the hallway checking him out.

But, we agreed to be friends. Going to the dance with him, what kind of signal would that send? I was caught between a rock and a hard place. I sorta kinda liked him, but what did *sorta, kinda like* mean?

"Oh, we don't have to go as girlfriend and boyfriend or anything," he said, taking some of the pressure off. I'm sure he saw from my distressed face that I wasn't up for that.

"We don't?" I asked, unsure what it would mean.

"No, just two best friends going to the dance to have a good time."

"Okay, yeah. That sounds good."

⤞⚬⤝

Of course when we got home and talked to Mom about it later that night she went off.

"No, y'all are not going to no dance. Last time there was some party at school, I had to leave my job to get Yancy out of trouble and then go and get York out of jail!"

"But what did that have to do with me, Ma?" I asked, not wanting to be penalized for something that I didn't do.

"And I learned my lesson, Ma. Come on, I'm not going to get into trouble like that," Yancy added.

"Ma, what about me?" York asked. "Can I go?"

"Boy, please, you told me you were gon' be at the party last time and you left to go to some store to steal something. Are you kiddin'? No, all three of you guys—home, home, home."

My two brothers looked at me as Mom went over to load the dishwasher. Obviously, I had no influence. Their crazy stares showed me they thought I did.

"You go talk to her," York said.

"You know you wanna be there with Myrek," Yancy added, looking pitiful. "It's going to be embarrassing if we can't go to the little Valentine's dance."

"Ma," I said as I went over and stroked her back.

"Yasmin, don't even give me that little sad puppy dog stare. It is not gon' work, girl. How much does it cost to go to the dance anyway?" she asked, quickly letting me know I had a chance.

"Girls get in free, and it wasn't me that got in trouble last time it was *those* two."

"Thanks, sis," Yancy said, rolling his eyes.

York put up his fist when Mom turned her back. I could only smile at the two of them. It wasn't my fault they were knuckleheads; I was not gonna vouch for the fact that if she did let them go to the dance this time that they wouldn't trip again. I could only speak for myself and I had been doing what I needed to. I pulled my grades up some, and I had been babysitting Randi and Dante for Miss Sandra, without pay.

"Ma, you can't let her go and not let us go. We gotta keep an eye on her," Yancy said.

"What do you mean, keep an eye on her?" Mom asked.

"She's going with Myrek," Yancy said, calling himself telling on me.

"No, we're just friends, Ma," I said, rolling my eyes at him.

"All right, all right, Yas, I know you and Myrek are just friends," she said.

"Boys, if you go, what kind of money do you need?"

"I still got money from Uncle John," Yancy explained.

"Um, yeah, me too," York said, knowing that he was hiding something; namely, money from Bone.

"Okay," Mom said to York in a surprised tone, knowing that he usually was the first person to spend all the money that he got his hands on.

Even I didn't really believe that. I knew that Bone was paying him. However, I couldn't tell it. So I zipped my lip.

"You know what? Let's just forget all that. You guys got your money. Everybody deserves a second chance. I'm gonna let you all go, and I'll be there at eight o'clock to pick you up."

Yancy said, "But, Ma, the dance starts at six and it isn't over until nine."

"Take it or leave it. You'll have two hours—from six to eight."

Yancy knew he'd better quit while he was ahead or else we wouldn't be able to go at all.

Everybody at school couldn't wait for the week to fly by, and when Friday came, all the buzz was about the dance. My classmates, Nelson and Tony, hung around me that day.

"So you know you gotta dance with me," Nelson said.

"Uh huh, you gotta dance with me too," Tony replied.

Then they started going back and forth with each other talking about who would dance with me first. We'd only joked before as buddies. I didn't understand why they wanted to dance with me.

I said, "Okay, guys, sorry to bust your bubble, but I'm going with somebody else," I said, winking at them.

⊸◈⊱

Later that evening, Myrek and I found ourselves sitting on the bleachers. I wasn't worried about York or Yancy. I wasn't there to be their babysitters. Whatever they did was their business. I wanted to have a good time with my best friend but we seemed so disconnected—like we couldn't talk about what was really going on. He was looking to the left side of the room and I was looking to the right. We didn't want to look at each other. Finally, Nelson came over to us and said, "You ain't hit the dance floor none. Man, you need to go on and let me take her and show her a good time."

"I got this," Myrek said, swatting Nelson's hand away.

"You wanna dance?" Myrek asked me in front of Nelson.

I nodded. When we went out on the floor, a slower paced song started playing. The chaperones were everywhere to keep kids from getting too close, which was good because I wasn't into trying to act all grown.

"What's wrong?" I asked him, feeling like he was thousands of miles away.

"Forget it, forget it. It was stupid of me to think that we could come to this dance as friends." Myrek started walking away from me.

"Wait up," I said, following him off the crowded floor.

"You just want to be my friend, Yasmin, and I thought that was okay, but it's not all right."

"What? What do you want?" I asked.

"You really want to know?" Myrek asked.

"Yeah, I do," I said in a bewildered tone.

Then he leaned over and gave me a big kiss on my lips. He was so forceful with it that it didn't feel good at all. I didn't like what he'd done and he didn't even ask me, not that I would've said yes anyway. I didn't want to hurt his feelings but he had crossed the line. However, I was frozen just standing there, not knowing how to respond.

So I said, "What are you doing, Myrek?"

"I'm sorry. I'm sorry. Forget it, I shouldn't have done that."

"Yeah, you're right you shouldn't have. You didn't even ask me if you could kiss me. You could get me in trouble by doing what you did," I said not sounding happy about it at all.

He just stood there looking at me.

My heart felt like a fifty-pound weight was on it. He was my friend, and yet I was upset with him. I had to go and cool down.

⋙⋘

I went over to the concession stand to get something to drink and I ran into Veida and Yancy. His hands were all around her waist.

"Are you crazy, boy?" I said as I thumped him upside his head. "You gon' get in trouble all over again. Teachers are monitoring this and you're not supposed to touch anybody."

They just laughed. Ugh, my brother was so gullible. I wished that I could knock some sense into him.

"You worried 'bout me, you better go check out York. Looks like he's over in the corner doin' something suspect."

"You are lying," I said to Yancy.

"Veida, tell her," he said.

She nodded. "Your brother looks like he's doing something crazy for real. For real."

"Why didn't you say something to him?" I huffed.

"Like I care if he gets into trouble. He thinks he knows everything. He wants to be with Dad so bad anyway. Let him get locked up."

"Yancy, I can't believe you're saying this," I said.

When I walked over toward York, I couldn't tell exactly what he was doing. But the way his pants were sagging, I saw what looked like a gun, and now a hundred-pound weight was on my heart. This was crazy. Why would York have a gun?

I went back over to where Yancy was and said, "Look, I need you to come with me and talk to York for real. He is doin' some stupid stuff."

"I just told you he was," Yancy said nonchalantly. "Don't you see, I'm with my girl? You know Ma is coming to get us before the dance is actually over, so stop bugging me."

Veida upset me further when she said, "Just because you're not with Myrek doesn't mean the two of us don't want to spend time together."

"Yeah, where is Myrek anyway?" Yancy asked. "You need to be trying to find him and stop messing with York. York's a big boy."

I said, "Forget it, Yancy, I don't even know why I thought you'd care."

"Good point, cause I don't," he shot back.

Yancy and Veida laughed at me and went back to the dance floor. When I looked in the same corner where I had just seen York, he was gone.

All right, Lord, I prayed, as I frantically searched around the gym. *Where is York? My brother is losing his mind. I hope he's not trying to sell drugs, or doing something else crazy, but if he is, he's not going to listen to me. It looks like he might even have a gun. I don't know if it's real or what! I just need You to help me find him before he does something stupid. Lord, please give me the words to say so that he won't go off 'cause I'm trying to help him. Oh, and Myrek, please let us work all that out too. I thought we'd come to some understanding that we were just going to be friends and out of the blue, he kisses me. See, I'm trying to do right and it's just so hard. Help, Father. Please. Help!*

Then all of a sudden, I saw York slapping hands with some boy like they had just come to some agreement. I went over to him and saw even more of the gun than I did the first time. York was into more than he could handle.

"What is this?" I asked as I touched it and tried to pull up his pants.

"Girl, you better watch it." York said, glaring at me.

"Why do you even have it, York? This is crazy! Is it real or what?" I knew that there were guns that looked real and weren't. But I didn't know the difference.

"Don't worry if it's real or not. It's my business. I gotta protect myself. I got a few things on me that's pretty valuable."

"Valuable? You mean drugs? Yancy told me that he thought you were over here up to somethin'!"

York started talking all tough. "Yancy needs to mind his own business. I got this."

I asked, "Are you selling drugs at the Valentine's party?"

"Yasmin, quit acting like everything is so good. Yeah, Ma got her little job and she getting a small paycheck, but it ain't enough. We still poor. We still strugglin' and I still need to do what I need to do to add a little extra to the household."

I said, "But sellin' drugs, York? Come on, man, you care about people too much to get them strung out."

"If people stupid enough to take it, then that's on them. I'm not nobody's parent."

"Yeah, but you're a boy who cares."

"Naw, you got me confused with Myrek. He came over here practically cryin' saying you ain't gon' wanna do nothing but be just friends. He needs to move on to somebody else."

Tearing up, I said, "I can't believe you said that, York. You know I care about him."

"He and I agreed we were gonna be friends. Now he's reneging on that. How am I supposed to feel? I should be the one all upset."

"Yeah, but you made him agree to something he didn't really wanna do. That boy has serious dreams about you at night, you know what I'm saying?"

I so wanted to walk away from York. He was turning this whole thing on me and Myrek when I came to get him straight about himself. Selling drugs, carrying a gun on school property. Obviously he wasn't thinking at all.

"I can't let you do this," I said to him boldly.

Then I turned around and started to walk away. He grabbed my arm really hard. So hard it hurt.

"Wait, Yasmin, you need to think about what you're saying.

What you gonna do, go snitch to the principal or something?"

"I don't know what I'm gonna do, York. I don't know."

Just then a chaperone came over and said, "Okay, what's going on here? Aren't you two siblings? Seems like you all are having a dispute that's getting a little too loud. Take your hands off of her."

"Me and my sister, we all good," York said, letting me go. "Everything's straight."

And the gun was still showing. I tugged on my shirt hard so he'd get the message. I started talking with the chaperone, trying to distract her when York didn't seem to understand what I was saying.

"We're fine. Just brother and sister stuff. Sorry it got too loud," I said.

"All right, I just wanted to make sure nothing crazy was going on." Then the chaperone left.

"Good looking out, sis, that's what I'm talkin'bout," York said in my ear.

"I'm not gonna let you ruin your life, York."

"Look, you gotta let me do this my way. You go and tell Ma or the principal and it'll be far worse. I'm just gon' do what I gotta do and I'll be out, all right? I'm puttin' away a little stash. I got this. You need to move on like none of this ever happened. Trust me when I say I don't need you getting involved with my business. Right now it's just easier to forget."

Chapter 6

Angrier
Every Moment

"The only reason I'm going to this LIGHT meeting is because they have off the chain refreshments," Perlicia said to Asia, Veida, and me as we headed to the library for the meeting.

"I hear that. I'm really not trying to hear what they have to say either," Veida said to her as they slapped hands.

I was actually surprised when Asia walked beside me. "I don't know. I got a lot out of the meeting a couple of weeks ago. I can't really talk to Perlicia about it, because she just laughs at me. I'm pretty scared about just diving in and having sex. AIDS is out there, pregnancy is out there, and some guy just dumping me because all he wanted to do was hit it and leave could destroy my life. I'm just not going to be the one."

I really couldn't believe she was saying what she was saying to me. This was the girl who just seemed so shallow most of the time, following right behind Perlicia's sinking footsteps. But now she was standing her ground, thinking for herself, and it was pretty moving to me.

"What, Yasmin? Why are you looking at me like that?" Asia asked, seeing by my expression that I was completely caught off guard.

"I'm just surprised. That's all, Asia."

"Actually, I am too. You mind if I sit with you?" she asked.

"No. That's cool," I said.

Unfortunately, Perlicia and Veida followed us, and they started laughing at what other people were wearing. It was just so obnoxious. Both of them had older sisters so they could get their style right, and they had access to more clothes too. Some of us were just doing the best we could with the little money we had.

"If y'all gon' sit here and talk about other people, y'all can move somewhere else," Asia said, surprising me once again.

"Ohh! Let's hush up before we get into any trouble," Perlicia said, making fun of Asia.

Asia started getting frustrated, so I leaned over and said, "Girl, you've got to learn how to ignore them like I do."

She smiled. "Thanks, Yasmin."

"Asia, I apologize because I always saw you through Perlicia's eyes, and I gave you a hard time because of it. It's like I have just wiped my eyes, and I can see that you're really cool."

Asia confessed, "Naw, I made it hard for you to get to know me. You're really a cool person, Yasmin."

"Well, hello ladies," Mrs. Newman said, coming into the library.

I was happy about that because I was starting to feel a little uneasy about the sweet comments Asia was making. It wasn't that I didn't want them or anything, but it was already hard enough that she was changing right before my very eyes. I didn't need her to dig too much. I wasn't trying to be let down as quickly as I let my guard up.

"The last time we were together, I know it was pretty emotional hearing from the three speakers, but we certainly hope that you got something out of each of the talks. Dating and sex are very serious issues. Miss Bennett and I hope that this LIGHT group will shine bright, calling out the turmoil, chaos, and pressure coming at you."

"We're concerned about another matter going on in our school, which is affecting a lot of our kids," Mrs. Newman said as she stepped toward Miss Bennett. "And that's all this gang initiation business. Kids are afraid of going to class, afraid of getting jumped, and feeling intimidated to do all kinds of things. So we brought a parent in to talk to you this time and to share her experiences with her daughter. Mrs. Washington, please come forward."

We all clapped. The lady didn't look old, but she had a worn out look. She clearly had been through a lot.

"Well, this isn't easy for me to speak in front of a group about my daughter. She has pretty much run away from home. A couple years ago everything was normal. She was an eighth-grader at another middle school in the county. I didn't have the best job, so I couldn't afford to give her all of the fancy stuff she wanted, and she was getting picked on for not having much.

"I have another daughter who was in the sixth grade at the time and she knew that her sister was unhappy. I didn't know she was crying all of the time because I was working. Some gang girls approached her and offered her protection, money, and a good time. Because I wasn't there to give her comfort and honestly wasn't aware that anything was wrong, she took them up on their offer. Now, she's gone."

"So, you don't know where your daughter is?" Veida asked.

"No, I don't. I don't even know how she's doing. I don't know anything. As a mom it's killing me, but I should have been more involved. I'm here today to tell you guys that your parents love you. They might not have all the right answers. They might not seem like they're cool. However, if you've got some heavy stuff holding you down and people showing you an easy way out, go to your parents or some responsible adult and talk to them."

"My parents don't want to listen," Perlicia shouted out.

Showing a lot of emotion, Mrs. Washington said, "If you have any siblings in trouble, don't sit by idly watching. My other daughter regrets every night that she didn't tell me what was going on with her sister. Hear me, if someone you know is hanging with the wrong crowd, then tell somebody before it is too late!"

The words that she spoke sent chills up and down my spine. It was like I was breaking out in a cold sweat or something. I really knew I needed to do *something* about York, but I just didn't know what. He told me to forget it, and I thought it would be best to do just that. But it was like God had sent this lady to talk to me and let me know I couldn't just forget it. I had to do something. I had to stand up, if my brother wasn't going to stand up for himself. I needed to make sure that we didn't lose him. Even if he hated me for the rest of my life, at least he'd be alive. I'd already lost one brother. Yeah, I was definitely going to do something.

⚜

My mom gave Mrs. Newman permission to drop me off after the LIGHT meeting. I guess it was twofold. One, she could make sure I wasn't into anything crazy and, two, Mom couldn't get off work. Her new job had her working from nine to five and we got out exactly at five.

"You're kind of quiet, Yasmin. Do you want to talk about anything?" Mrs. Newman asked me.

We were able to talk about so much. I really appreciated her starting the girls' group to help a lot of us seventh- and eighth-graders do better in life, but I knew what I had to do. I had to help York. I just didn't know how. Talking to her wasn't going to help me. When we pulled into my apartment complex and York was slapping hands with Bone, I couldn't hold back my disgust. They didn't notice her car at first, but when they did, they stared us down.

"I know your brother is not hanging with that hoodlum Bone?" Mrs. Newman asked.

"Yeah, it looks like the talk was right on time for me, huh? Like my mom doesn't have enough to deal with, she's got to deal with York losing his mind too."

"Has she tried to talk to him? Does she know he's hanging with these characters?"

"She's working all of the time. She doesn't know what he's doing."

"Well, Yasmin, I don't want to put any pressure on you. If you want me to talk to your mom so you can stay out of it, I don't mind speaking to her."

"Naw, this ain't, I mean, *isn't* about you. Honestly, my mom is so tired and stressed that I don't want to bother her."

Then Mrs. Newman said, "Well, I'll be praying about it and you do the same, Yasmin."

I quickly thanked her and got out of the car. I was glad Mrs. Newman didn't lecture me but said she'd pray. I had heard the lady loud and clear at the LIGHT meeting. Now I just needed the strength to go to bat for my brother.

Lord, I prayed, *I know every time You turn around it's me asking for something. Something crazy is going on in my family. I know You are aware of it already. Though I have been consistently praying to You over the last six months, I'm confused. What am I supposed to do about my brother? York won't listen to me. Please show me the way, Lord. Amen.*

All of a sudden, the phone rang. It was my dad!

An operator asked if I'd accept the charges and I excitedly said yes.

"Pumpkin, is that you?" Dad asked.

"Yeah, Dad, it's me."

I hadn't spoken to him since Thanksgiving.

"I don't have too much time to talk. I'm on my free time now. What's going on? You got my letter?"

"Yeah, I did. Thanks for reaching out to me like that."

"I'm just sorry it took me so long to put my thoughts down on paper. I'm really sorry, you know I love you, Jas . . . Yasmin."

"Dad, you don't know my name?"

"I'm sorry. I just can't believe I'm talking to my daughter and getting a little tongue-tied. Where are your brothers?"

"I don't even know where Yancy is, but I need to talk to you about York."

Excitedly, my dad said, "My boy! What's up with him?"

I really didn't want to alienate my brother by driving a wedge between him and the only person he really respected. Why did I have to be the responsible one? Where was Yancy so that he could help me explain this? He should have been home and he wasn't.

"Dad, he's hanging out with a guy that I know is into illegal stuff."

"What do you mean?"

"Drugs, terrorizing people, carrying guns; he was even questioned in a murder. The guy has a really horrible reputation. He's the same one who said that Jeff owed him money. And York has been packing at school, Dad."

"What? Where is York at now? Put him on the phone!" he shouted.

"He's not here and I know he's gonna hate me for talking to you. But Dad, this lady came to our after-school program today, and she was talking about losing her daughter to a gang. The girl ran away from home. After hearing that, I just had to do something, even if it cost me my relationship with York."

"It's okay, sometimes folks need to get mad. You talk to your mom?"

"She's got too much on her right now and you're the only person York goes around here talking about. You're his hero, Dad."

"What is he trying to do? Come to prison too? What is that boy thinking?" Dad said.

"I don't know, but you're really the only one that can get through to him."

Just then the door opened and York walked in. I felt like I was going to throw up. I really didn't want to deal with him.

"Who is that you talkin' to all quiet? I know you and Myrek talk on the phone whispering love notes into each other's ear and everything. Ain't no need to try and front for me, sis."

My heart sank. I was helping him out, but I knew he wouldn't see it like that.

York grabbed the phone. "Myrek, you live right next door, I know my mom told you we couldn't have no company, but . . . my sister needs to loosen up, tryin' to be all up in my business."

I was standing so close to York, I could hear my father's raised voice.

York said, "Dad?"

"Dad, what's up? You know I was playing about all of that, right? Yas is a good girl and you'll be proud of her."

Then York put him on speakerphone.

He said, "Boy, don't no boy need to come over and see your sister. You have lost your mind! Yeah, and don't you go and try to corrupt her either."

"I'm just playing, Dad, for real."

"The question is, son, are you good? Your sister told me . . . "

I couldn't believe what I'd just heard Dad say. I tried to walk away and not listen to anymore of the conversation so I went to my room. No matter how I felt, it was out of my hands now.

Moments later, I came back and Dad was still talking. York mouthed the words *I hate you.* My eyes just filled up with water. I had gone out of my way to protect him. Now, I had to deal with the fallout.

"You selling, you packing, you running with that no good dude?" Dad asked.

"Pops, let me explain. You would be proud of me—I'm helpin' Ma out."

Dad shot back, "That is not your responsibility. I've got my brother handling some of that."

"Dad, the only reason we got cable is because I got the hookup, okay?"

"And everything that comes easy ain't right, son. Why do you think I'm behind bars?"

"I don't need you to worry about me. I've got this," York said.

"No son, you're gonna promise me right now that you're gonna stop it and walk away from all of this no good business."

"Dad, you know it ain't that easy. You can't just back out of the game whenever you want. I'm picking up what Jeff left off owing."

"You're going to break your mom's heart if you get locked up. I don't know if I can take that either. If you learned anything from me, it should've been that the fast life is not the life you want to live. You're smart enough to find a way to quit hangin' out with this Bone guy. If you can't do it, call your Uncle John. You don't need no parts of it. I need your word!"

"Dad, you know it's not that easy. And Uncle John ain't in Jacksonville. He can't do nothin'."

After the conversation with Dad, York looked like he wanted to hit me. As bad as he was, he wasn't crazy. Instead, he hit the couch. I knew I'd opened Pandora's box and I couldn't close it now.

"York, please talk to me," I begged him.

"Like I have anything to say to you. I told you to forget what you saw, but you just had to stick your nose in my business."

"It's not just your business. You might hate me, but I love you. I already lost one brother and I ain't going to lose another one, okay?" I said completely emotional as I got up in his face. "I'm sorry!"

"Yeah, right!"

Then the front door opened and it was Yancy.

"What are y'all yelling about?" he asked.

"Where you been?" York asked.

Yancy answered, "Out with Ma, shopping."

"Shopping for what?" I asked.

"Just stuff, man, Quit asking me a hundred questions!" Yancy said.

"Why are you bein' so stingy with information?" York asked angrily.

Yancy said, "Since you're so nosey, here's some information for you: Ma is going out with Mr. Mike. They're talking about the specifics right now."

York said, "I bet you're happy about that! Ma don't need to be with somebody who's just as bad off as we are!"

"Are you kidding?" Yancy said. "At first I didn't know if I liked the idea but now I'm okay with it. You want her to get back with Dad, and look where he is. What has he done for us? Oh, I forgot, that's the only thing that you think is honorable. The crazy way you're acting, you're going to land there."

York pushed Yancy. Yancy used to be a little passive, but he got up and pushed my tougher brother back. The next thing I knew, the two of them were tussling all over the couch.

Living in the ghetto was heartache enough. There never seemed to be enough money to do too much of anything. I didn't know if all of the stress made the people who lived there more and more agitated, but that certainly seemed like the case for my family. It seemed like there was never a happy moment about anything.

All of a sudden Mom walked in the door and said, "York! Get off of him."

York got off Yancy and hit him one more time. "You *would* take his side. You know what, Ma, I'm sick of you always thinking that I'm the one doing somethin' wrong. I'm tired of Yasmin, who can't keep her nose in her own business, and your precious other son gets on my last nerve. You can have it all, I'm leavin'!"

"Boy, you are not goin' nowhere," Mom yelled out.

"Whatever, Ma! This dysfunctional, po' family doesn't work for me. Bone is the only one who cares."

I couldn't believe what I was hearing. This was exactly what the lady was talking about earlier today. Why did York think that we didn't care? I only told Dad what he was up to because I cared.

York went to the bedroom and started packing his clothes.

Mom said, "Listen here, boy, you are not takin' one thing from this house. I'm the one who's taken care of your ungrateful self. Sit down! I said, you ain't going nowhere!"

York blew past her.

"You walk out of this house, York, and you are to NEVER come back!" Mom said as I saw veins popping out in her neck.

"Let him go, Ma. Let him go!" Yancy shouted.

"Don't worry, I'm out!" York said as he opened the door and slammed it on his way out.

I slid to the floor and cried. It was chaos around me. I couldn't believe all that had happened in just a couple of minutes. Every time I would try and say something pleasant to the people around me it would backfire, and they were getting angrier every moment.

Chapter 7

Blower
of Smoke

ord, You just gotta help me. I can't lose another son!"
Mom declared after York stormed out the door.

I had been reading many books at school to keep up with the quota that Miss Bennett gave us. None of the drama in any of them related to all of the real-life problems that I had to face. My mom was living with three teenagers. Each of us was strong-willed and had our own opinions. But she was still the mother and my two brothers seemed to forget that crucial point.

Yancy didn't even appear to be phased that York had left. But mom headed off down the street after him. For some reason, I just believed my brother would finally get some sense, turn around, and come back. But when that didn't happen, I jogged behind my mother.

"You're not gonna be able to catch him. He's probably going to hang with Bone," I said to her.

"Bone?" she said disapprovingly. "That little toothpick thug who dropped out of school and has been causin' all kinds of trouble? I know your brother is not out here hanging out with him!"

"Ma, it's such a long story," I said.

She slowed down and touched my arm. "I hurt York and I know he's upset with me, Yasmin. You guys have to come to me when you have problems. You have to talk to me. You need to let me in on why you feel your world is so difficult."

"But, Ma, you got your own stuff that weighs you down and now you got this new job. Finally, you're smiling. No one wants to upset you again. So we just go about our way, doing our thing, hoping to please you. I just think . . . nothing, forget it. Go get York, please."

"Girl, talk to me. Tell me what you need to say."

I mumbled, "I think we need more guidance."

"Well, that's what I'm tryin' to tell you. I wanna be there for you guys, but I can't if you don't open up to me."

Myrek and his dad pulled up beside us.

"Yvette, I'll pick you up in— is everything okay?" Mr. Mike asked.

"No, it's not. I can't make it for dinner, Mike. Something came up. Listen, right now I really need a ride, I'm too nervous to drive my car. Yasmin and I are trying to catch up with York," she said, pointing in the direction we thought York went.

"What's going on?" he asked.

"I don't feel like explaining right now. I just need to catch my son. I gotta save my family. I'm doing the best I can with these kids—tryin' to be mom and dad."

He said, "All right, all right, hop in. Come on, let's go and get him."

Mr. Mike said, "I know it's tough, Yvette. Especially with that hard-headed York, who thinks he knows every—"

"I don't want to hear that about my son right now. I know he's strong-willed and hanging with the wrong crowd, but he's still my son and I just can't lose him. I just can't, Mike."

There was so much tension in the air with my mom being all upset and Mr. Mike driving fast that Myrek and me didn't have to worry about addressing our own issues. I knew he was still upset with me about the whole kissing incident. Sometime soon one of us was gonna have to bring up that whole thing so we could talk about it. But now, it just wasn't the time.

"Hey, son, your mom wants to talk to you," Mr. Mike said as he pulled up beside York.

"Man, please, don't call me son!" York said.

"Ma, you need to tell him he ain't my dad, seriously. I ain't tryin' to disrespect him, but I mean, you know, come on, Ma. I'm not going back to the house, so y'all can just get on back in that car and leave," York said hastily.

"You need to settle down and listen to her," Mr. Mike said, getting out of the car and approaching York.

York shouted, "I don't need you to help me talk to my mom!"

"Let me just talk to him," Mom said.

"Fine. Let me get out the way and just let y'all do whatever," Mr. Mike said, looking at my mom like she misunderstood where he was coming from.

"This is just a hot mess," I said to Myrek as we sat in the car.

In an uncaring tone, Myrek said, "Sometimes you just got to let people find their own way. And things ain't gonna always go the way you want them to, Yasmin. I have that learned, even though we are in Florida, we don't live in Disney World."

What he was saying sounded like it had something to do with us, but I was too focused on York and my family to try and figure it out. I definitely felt like Myrek's words applied to York and Mom and I had to take hold of his words. It wasn't for me to make my brother come home. But then I realized that I knew the One who could.

So I bowed my head and prayed, *You know, Lord, this is hard. Work all this out for my family, please. We need You so badly.*

Mom and York talked for a few more minutes and then she said to Mr. Mike, "Thanks for your help."

"Yeah, no problem. I'm glad I could help somehow, Yvette." Mr. Mike then told Mom they could grab something to eat at another time.

Mom motioned for me to step out of the car. She said that it would be best for her, York, and me to walk back to our apartment and talk along the way.

When Myrek and his dad drove away, I felt like there was still unresolved stuff between our two families.

❧

If there was ever a time that Mom needed a break from us kids, this was it. "Ma, you still could've gone to dinner with Mr. Mike," I said.

"Yasmin, my children come first. I know what I need to do. This wasn't the time for me to go out."

Mom continued, "York, I can't have you leave my house and run away thinking that I don't love you with all my heart and soul. I care about you, boy. I care about Yancy. I care about Yasmin. We just need to work on us right now. We've got to find a way to be the family that we're supposed to be. The Lord can help us do that. I know we both said a whole bunch of things. Some of which we can't even remember. I know it may seem comfortable in those streets right now. But York, don't nobody love you like we do."

"Ma, you just saying words so I'll come back home. You don't really mean all that." He looked away.

She hugged him. "You know, boy, you may be a triplet but you're definitely one of a kind, and I love you."

"I love you too, Ma," he said as he wrapped his arms tightly around her.

I clasped my hands together and inwardly shouted, *Thank You, Lord!*

⟆⟐⟅

Most of the teachers at our middle school were African American. We had a few white teachers. And the one teacher everybody loved was Miss Neal. She truly cared for each of her students and wanted to make sure that we understood every bit of history; particularly, the past that dealt with African Americans and slavery.

"I gave you all an assignment at the beginning of the month," Miss Neal said. "Instead of writing a paper, we are going to talk about the Civil War and what it means to you. Then I want you all to give me an example of how the Civil War equates with things going on in your own lives. Anyone want to go first?"

I sort of dozed off at that point; this was first period and I hadn't been getting much sleep. Though York was back, he was sleeping in the living room on the couch. My two brothers weren't coexisting very well. So much tension was in our small space.

When my mom was at work, life was much worse.

"Okay, okay. I see some of you guys are writing down things and some are talking. You aren't even prepared for this assignment at all. The next person I call on better be able to give me the history of the Civil War or the class will take a quiz," she said. The kids let out a bunch of groans throughout the classroom. "Yasmin Peace, let's go."

I so hated being called on, even though I had read the assignment. I bowed my head and collected my thoughts.

Trying hard to wake up, I stood and said, "The Civil War was a fight between the northern states that were part of the Union and the southern states that made up the Confederacy. It started in 1861 because after Abraham Lincoln was elected president in 1860, he wanted to stop the spread of slavery. The folks in the South just weren't going for that, so they seceded from the Union. In 1861, the Confederate Army took over Fort Sumter in Charleston, South Carolina. And then the war was on. It was long and bloody. Over six hundred thousand men, if you combined both sides, lost their lives. Over a million more were injured. The South finally gave in when General Lee surrendered in 1865 to the North."

"Wow," Miss Neal said. "I am really impressed."

"Yeah, no test!" someone yelled out.

Not letting me off the hook just yet, she continued, "Okay, okay —well, Miss Peace, tell me how this relates to something in your life now."

"I think everybody knows that I'm a triplet. I can understand the Civil War in a personal way. The Union at one time included everybody. And not to let y'all in on my family business, but when my two brothers go at it, they pull apart what's supposed to be one.

Feelings get hurt. It is very personal and it gets ugly. But at the end of the day we try to come together and be a family. Sort of like what happened when the South gave in to the North."

"That's awesome," Miss Neal said. "Anyone else?"

Asia raised her hand and said, "Yeah, I'm sort of like Yasmin. That's how I relate to the Civil War. Though the North didn't care about slavery, or didn't mind if we were free, the South depended on African Americans at that time. We made up a third of the population in the South. African Americans picked cotton and were just needed to make things work.

"I think today we're still needed to make things work. And as I think back on what the Civil War means to me, I'm just excited that people fought for human rights. And at the end of the politics, the good side won out. I pray every day that the good in my life wins."

"Very good," said Miss Neal. "Next?"

My friend Nelson, who was always so silly, surprised me when he said, "Yeah, I learned that so many people died in the war. I know that people gave their lives so that I could have more, be free, and come to school to get an education. And I know people think that I waste a lot of my time at school not really trying, but when I read stories like this, I know that deep down some people didn't want me to have it. Now, I'm motivated to do better."

"I love the self-reflection some of you guys have been doing as you think about the Civil War and you take yourself back to that place in time when African Americans had no voice. Much has been given with the Emancipation Proclamation that happened in 1864. Slaves were freed, and in some ways, so were their ancestors."

I sat back smiling. Like Nelson had just said, we were now free to do great things. We could realize the dreams of those who had lived before us.

Miss Neal continued, "Class, do not waste your time. There is so much to be made up for."

She had all of our attention at that point. The Civil War just wasn't about past history. I couldn't even worry about seeing six hundred thousand people gone. Sometimes we read the textbook and take in just enough to pass the test. But if we went deeper, put ourselves in that place, and tried hard to imagine what it was like— what people gave up and sacrificed—then we could be inspired.

She closed and said, "Boys and girls, hold high the torch and continue making your ancestors in heaven proud."

⚜

Later after school, York asked, "So you gon' go with me, right?" He was referring to Myrek's basketball game. I was in such a dilemma. There was no way I could say no, but I would be so un-comfortable. I guess York was going to be too. "They're taking a pep bus over there, but we have to ride home with Myrek's dad," York said. It was no secret Myrek's dad was trying to be nice to York, but York wasn't going to make that easy at all. Yancy couldn't go to the game because he was staying after school to get ready for the science fair.

"Myrek is my boy. He wants me to be there," York said. "Ma said it's cool. I know you want to support Myrek."

I responded, "Please, I don't even know if he wants me there."

"Wait, there he is right there," York said as Myrek passed us in the hallway.

"Hey! You don't want my sister at your game?" York asked.

"Why you gotta ask him like that?" I said, elbowing York.

"Your sister's a big girl. She goes where she wants. Trust me, I don't want her to do anything that she doesn't want to," Myrek said, looking away.

York tried to get his attention, but clearly Myrek seemed uninterested in me. "What's up here? Girl, you should support him. What else you gon' go home and do? All you do every day is study. Your grades are already up."

With frustration, I gave in. "I'm going, York . . . okay, I'm going."

Myrek was just sort of standing there. It was weird that we lived so close to each other but avoided each other so much. On the bus in the morning, he was in the back and I was in the front. After school, I didn't have to see him because he was at basketball practice; I was either at home or with my LIGHT group.

Breaking the tension, he said, "Look, I'm sorry about a couple of weeks ago, okay? I shouldn't have kissed you at the dance. I talked with my dad about it and he said that's not how a young man should handle a situation. I shouldn't be physical with you at our age.

"I thought I could be your friend without feeling a certain way about you. My dad said that now as we're getting older, we'll have different feelings about the opposite sex, but that we have to be careful about our behavior— I gotta go. I'll see you after the game. But again, you didn't have to come. I'm not expecting nothing from you but friendship," Myrek said as he jogged away.

It was good that we now had the air clear.

When I was in the stands cheering him on, it was just genuine. Though our friendship had experienced some ups and downs, I felt we could still be good friends. I wanted him to succeed at his dreams. He worked hard at getting his shot back and he was awesome. The boy shot twenty-five points before halftime.

⚜

"You want something to drink?" York asked, walking over to me.

"I don't have any money," I said. He had a slick grin on his face that told me he did.

"What, you tryin' to act like my little money is dirty? I haven't been hanging out with Bone and 'em. I still have some of the change from Uncle John, okay?"

"All right," I said to him as we went over to the concession stand.

"Wait, is that your girl?" York asked me as he turned my face to the left.

I was stunned at what I saw. Veida was hugged up with some guy we didn't know.

"I thought she was all into your brother?" York said, trying to be funny as if Yancy was no kin of his. "Who is that she's with?"

"You know what? This is her old school. I can't believe her!" I said to York.

York said, "She's holdin' his hand all tight—standing on her tippy toes and laughing in his face."

I said, "Wait till I tell Yancy."

"Don't tell him nothin', Yasmin."

"Of course I'm going to tell him. And I'm hoping he's gonna tell me that he's not interested in her anymore. At least that would explain why Veida is in this boy's face."

"Uh, hold up, sis. Let him find out on his own. He don't like you in his business."

"I can't believe you, York," I said, wanting to take the nachos and throw them in my brother's hateful face. "All that Ma's been going through and you two have still been feuding over what exactly? Power? Position? Who can hold out the longest without saying I'm sorry? Grow up."

"Let him deal with this. Stay out of it. It's just like everything that happened to me. The next time Dad calls, are you gonna tell him this too?"

"Oh, I knew you wouldn't let that one go, York."

"I'm just saying, Yasmin, we're not babies. I don't agree with everything going on in your life."

"What are you talking about? I'm not even doing anything."

"You're leading Myrek on."

"That is so not true! I told you that we had agreed to be just friends. Talk about staying out of somebody's business."

"Well, that's what I'm saying, Yasmin. See how hot and bothered you gettin' about it? How you think Yancy's gonna take it when you call and tell him the girl he likes is playin' him? He's gonna resent you. And if you got an issue with me and him not speaking, you ain't gon' be able to deal with it if he ain't speaking to you. I'm tellin' you, Yasmin, you just need to let it go. You can't fix everything for everybody. You can't even fix your own life or your own friends. Veida was your girl at one time. You sure know how to pick 'em. But do whatever you want. I'm going back to watch the game."

I was standing there so upset. Some of what York said was true and some was a bunch of nonsense. I was just so mad at him and so mad at Veida. I could just about see steam coming out of my ears. I was really upset and practically a blower of smoke.

Chapter 8

Other
Than Me

I just stood there, looking at Veida all into a guy other than my brother Yancy.

"Okay, I had a change of heart," York tapped me on the shoulder and said.

"Really?" I asked.

"I got my issues with Yancy, but I can't let him go out like this."

"So we're gonna tell him when we get home?" I asked.

"Naw, we're gonna go talk to her now," York said.

Before I could question his decision, we were headed over to her. Veida couldn't even see us coming because her back was turned. York touched her shoulder and she looked like she'd seen a ghost when she saw us.

"No need to jump and act all nervous. What's done in the dark always comes to light," York said to Veida.

"Who are they?" A dude with a cast on his arm asked her as he practically looked down on us like we were trash or something.

"These are my um . . . my um . . ."

"Don't even worry about explaining," I said to Veida as she stumbled all over her words.

I didn't know if she was embarrassed in front of her high society friend because we looked like we didn't fit in or if she was still choked up over the fact that she got caught being in some guy's face. Either way, York and I weren't leaving her side without an explanation. Even though we were too young for serious relationships, Veida knew that Yancy thought the world of her, and she was only up in this boy's face because Yancy wasn't around. Nothing she could say would be good enough.

"You know, Yancy is gonna be so crushed," I said to her.

"Yancy, who's that?" the boy asked like he was upset. "Veida, what's up with this?"

"Yeah, Veida, why don't you tell him what's going on? Or do you need me to fill him in?" York responded condescendingly.

"Yasmin, can I talk to you for a second? Please, please can I talk to you for a second?" she said under her breath as she tried to nudge me over to the side.

"No, are you kidding? I don't know what kind of games you are playing Veida."

"This is my old school and I'm here . . ."

"—to see her man," the boy finished the sentence for her while he kissed her on the cheek.

"Oh, this is crazy," York said to him. "You and my brother think ya'll got dibs on the same chick."

The dude was not happy as he turned to Veida. "What's he talking about? Who is this other boy at your new school?"

Without answering, Veida dashed away. Then York and Veida's

friend just started talking about sports. *Leave it up to boys to do something like that*, I thought as I followed Veida.

"The sad thing, Veida, is that my brother really cares for you. And part of me really cared about you too. That's over though. I can't believe you've been playing us. Guess it just shows me who you truly are."

With watery eyes, she said, "I didn't mean to hurt Yancy. I care about him. It's just that . . ."

"I really don't want any explanations. As a matter of fact, I'm cool if you don't talk to me anymore, at all—ever again."

"Yasmin, please don't do this."

"See ya!" I said, throwing up my hand and firmly holding my cold nachos in the other.

When I got back to the stands York was acting all excited. The game was over and we had won. Myrek and our team threw down.

⋘⚬⋙

All the way home, Mr. Mike tried to make conversation, but all three of us were silent for various reasons. When we got out of the car, I said thank you to Myrek's dad and let Myrek know I was very proud of his performance. York dashed inside without saying a word.

We knew Yancy was in the bedroom, and as we headed back there, I asked, "You gonna tell him?"

"I really hope that you do, Yas, because I dunno how he's gonna take it. He might think I'm hatin' because we're mad at each other."

"But you'll go in there with me, right?" I asked.

He nodded. When we got to their room, York opened the door. Yancy was standing by the window.

I nudged York, "You tell him."

"No, just go ahead and tell him," York demanded.

When Yancy turned around, both York and I were stunned to see how sad he looked. "Nobody needs to tell me, all right? Veida confessed. She called me and told me the whole thing. York, I guess you want to say 'I told you so.'"

York said, "Man, I wouldn't do that. I'm just glad you know. I don't want no girl playin' you."

"Yeah, I know," Yancy said in an upset voice. "So you guys can get out and leave me alone now."

"We care about you, Yancy," I said, reaching out to hug him.

"I'm not a baby, Yasmin. Get back, please. I just need to deal with this on my own right now."

York coldly said, "Man, you better go on and get over her."

I picked up the nearest shirt and threw it at York's big mouth. York was never into just one girl. He didn't know what it felt like to have his heart crushed. And though a boy hadn't hurt me like that, I'd had plenty of friendship drama to empathize with Yancy.

"It ain't that easy, man. You never cared about a girl. You only care about yourself," Yancy said.

"That's what you want to believe. Believe it then," York said as he turned around to exit the room.

"Well, wait. Prove me wrong then, York. Stick around and tell me. Who else do you care about besides yourself?"

"I care about you, boy. I care about our family. All I'm saying is, it ain't worth it to get all upset over some girl. I ain't sayin' that it ain't a big deal," York explained in a slightly agitated tone.

I stood between them and said, "All right, ya'll, let's settle down. We're not mad at each other."

"Maybe that's just it though, Yasmin. I told you he was still upset with me," York explained.

"Boy, you're the one who wanted to walk out of the house. You're the one who moved out of our room. You're the one sleeping on the couch," Yancy said.

"So you got a problem with me," York replied as though he really didn't care to talk about it anymore.

Without letting Yancy respond, York slammed the door as he left their room. I knew Yancy was trying to be strong because my brother was in the room, and as soon as York's strong presence was gone, Yancy opened up to me.

"You're not the only one who got hurt here. Okay? I cared for her too," I said in a soft voice.

"Yeah, but you weren't stupid enough to put your heart out on the line. That's exactly what I did."

"We got into this together and we can get out of it," I said.

"She was just the first girl that I . . ."

He couldn't even finish it. Though he didn't look like he'd get over this anytime soon, I believed in my heart he'd pull through. I patted him on the back and just sat there. As York told me earlier, everything wasn't for me to fix, but that didn't mean I couldn't try to help my family go through things.

I didn't get to sit there too long because I heard York yelling out, "Yasmin, you got company at the door."

Honestly, I really hoped it wasn't Myrek. Even though we were back on good terms, I'd had enough drama with him already. He was the only one who lived close enough to come over and say anything to me. But I was surprised to see little Randi from next door. When she saw me coming toward the door, she ran and jumped into my arms.

"Yasmin, help me! Dante won't stop cryin' and I dunno what to do."

"It's okay, Randi. Go tell your mommy. Is she taking a nap? Do you need to wake her up?"

"No, she went to the store," Randi said with a mischievous grin like she was spilling a secret.

"Your momma left you home with the baby?" York overheard and asked.

"You gotta come now! Yasmin, he won't stop crying! Please." Randi tugged at my sleeve.

York pushed me out the door. "Go, I'll tell Ma where you are when she gets here."

"All right," I said to York.

When I got over there the place was a mess again. I couldn't even believe just a month ago my uncle, my brothers, and I had helped Miss Sandra get the place clean. Dante was on the floor crying. I ran over to him, picked him up, and instantly started rocking him.

"I think he fell out of his crib," Randi said. "I let down the bar because I wanted him to get out and play with me," she said, clearly not understanding what she'd done.

"But, sweetie, he's not able to step down like you. You're a big girl. He's just a baby. He needs your help."

"I'm sorry," she said as she grabbed my leg and squeezed it tight.

"Did your mommy say what time she was coming back?"

I got no response. Then I heard a loud noise; it was Randi's stomach growling. So, I went into the kitchen and opened the refrigerator. There were a couple cartons of milk. I was relieved, until I opened them up and the milk looked and smelled spoiled.

More forcefully this time, I said, "Randi, when did your mommy say she was coming back?"

Randi just hunched her shoulders. Then she rubbed her belly. I didn't know when was the last time the girl had had a meal.

"Did she say she was going to the store and someplace else too?" I continued my questioning. The baby would not stop wailing.

She shrugged her shoulders again. Why was I even asking a five-year-old these questions? And what in the world was her mom thinking?

"What about a pacifier, Randi?" I asked, thinking she'd know about that.

She nodded and dashed to his bed and came back with one. After I rinsed it off, I put it in his mouth and walked around with him. He was still crying.

"Maybe you should change his diaper," Randi said.

"Where are the diapers?"

"No more. My mommy went to get one," she said.

Sighing, I said, "So that's probably what's wrong with him."

I just started humming to little Dante, and when that didn't work, I prayed aloud. "Dear Lord, I got this baby in my arms and I know he is uncomfortable. His diaper is heavy and I can't change it. He doesn't want a pacifier and there is no milk to give him. Please, please, please help me. This isn't for me this time. Help me, Lord, so I can help him. Amen."

When I finished praying, remarkably, little Dante's eyes just started batting. He had calmed down. All the hollering must have worn him out because he drifted off to sleep.

"You're the bestest babysitter in the world," Randi said.

She jumped up and down. I had to take my free hand and put it toward my lips. Her stomping was making way too much noise.

"Don't say too much. We don't want to wake him, okay?" I pleaded.

"You better not put him down in that crib, 'cause he'll wake up again. It happens all the time with my mommy," she informed me as I started to lie him down.

I had been over there for fifteen minutes and her mom was nowhere in sight.

When someone knocked on the door I said, "Thank you, finally."

Thinking it was her mom needing help with the groceries, I opened it. It was my mom instead. With her hands on her hips and her foot tapping, she didn't appear happy.

"Yasmin, what is going on over here?"

"She's helping me babysit my brother," little Randi said.

"I can see that, sweetie, but where's your mommy?" Mom asked her in no joking mood.

Randi gave her infamous shoulder shrug. "I dunno."

"Sweetie, do you know what time she left?" Mom asked.

Randi lifted her shoulders again and said, "It was a long time ago. Barney was on. My mommy got a call and had to go real quick to get the diapers," Randi said without understanding that her mom still could have called someone or took them with her.

"Ma, what are we supposed to do?" I asked.

"I don't know, but her mother is becoming more and more

irresponsible," Mom whispered so that Randi couldn't hear. "This is just too much for two young babies."

I whispered back, "I found him on the floor."

"I hate this because I know how hard it is to be a single mother, but I told her if she had an emergency to at least check next door to see if one of us was home."

"Yasmin, you go on home and finish your homework. You went to that game so you could not have done it all. I bought some fried chicken. Take Randi with you."

My mom wrote a note for Miss Sandra.

Just as we got to the door, she came hustling in. "Randi, honey, I'm home."

"I can't believe you would leave this child and baby by themselves," my mom scolded.

"I know, Yvette. I just got caught up. I'm so tired. There's so much going on and it's just hard to do it all."

"I don't need to hear no excuses," my mom told her, eyeing the phone.

"You know I'm a good mother. I'm doing the best I can with these babies. Please don't call nobody on me. Who's gonna take care of them? Who's gonna love my babies like I can?" she pleaded.

"Well, you're not showin' that you love them that much, leaving them here to fend for themselves, girl! Your baby was on the floor."

Rolling her eyes at my mom she said, "Sometimes people need to keep their noses in their own business."

"Your daughter came to get my child for help, but since you think you got it—"

"I just want some chicken, Mommy," Randi interjected, tugging at her mom's short dress.

"I'm gonna feed your kids now," Mom said.

"And you might want to change the baby's diaper," she continued. "And since you ain't got none in your arms, safe to say you weren't at the grocery store. I suggest you go there for real now and get some."

Miss Sandra just hung her head and said thanks.

We left their apartment heading to ours to feed Miss Sandra's kids.

⚜

Randi and Dante were eating as if they hadn't had food in years. I asked, "What are you gonna do, Ma?"

"I don't know. I'm just going to pray right now. I don't want to see her lose her kids, but if she ain't doin' those babies no good maybe someone else can."

Then my mom looked at Randi and Dante and hunched her shoulders.

⚜

It was time for another LIGHT meeting. The year was flying by. I couldn't believe it was already the end of March. Pretty soon I would be on my way to high school.

I heard my name called over the intercom to come to the office, but I'd gone to get help with an algebra assignment and had forgotten. When I saw Mrs. Newman on the way to the meeting, I remembered.

Mrs. Newman said, "Hello, Miss Yasmin, I requested that you

come to my office this morning. What happened?"

"I'm sorry, Mrs. Newman, I was getting help with some algebra and I didn't remember until I just saw you."

"Okay. Well, today's session is going to be really deep."

"That's good. We need deep. You and Miss Bennett have been keeping it real," I said to her.

Mrs. Newman said, "I wanted to talk to you about it a bit beforehand, which is why I called you to my office, but now we're about to get started. So, it's okay."

Hmm . . . I wondered what she was going to tell me. But just then, Miss Bennett walked up and she and Mrs. Newman said that the meeting would start in a minute.

Asia approached me as I entered the library and said, "Hey, Yasmin."

"Hey, I haven't seen you around," I said.

"I'm just dealing with a lot," she said as she walked past me and sat down alone.

I can tell when people need their space. Before, she was much more talkative. Now her eyes looked like they held a lot of sorrow.

Miss Bennett began to ask for everyone's attention as Mrs. Newman approached the podium. I sat down and felt sick when I spotted Veida. I really despised seeing her there. She and Perlicia had become really good friends. Veida looked like she wanted to come over and speak to me, but I just looked away and thankfully she didn't move.

"Okay ladies, as the counselor in this school, a lot of you come to me with different issues. I've been really concerned that so many of you have been telling me that you're depressed. Without revealing any particular thing about anybody, collectively, I think we need to address depression in this group. In belonging to this group called LIGHT, you are young women who stand for something. You have a vision, and you can go far in life. You do not have to walk in darkness. Miss Bennett and I want you to know that you can continue to come and talk to us."

I wondered where Mrs. Newman was going with this speech of hers. She had stopped me in the hall and told me that our session would be deep, and now she was saying that students were depressed. What were we talking about? What was going on? And why would it affect me?

Mrs. Newman said, "The first young lady we chose to speak today considered taking her own life."

At that moment I almost choked. So that's what Mrs. Newman was gonna talk to me about. Yes, this was going to be really hard. The girl got up and started speaking. I couldn't even hear her. All I could think about was that this was about suicide. The girls were looking at me because I had lost someone in my family that very way. I started sweating under my arms profusely. It wasn't even that time of the month. I was just really uncomfortable and wanted to leave. I turned around and grabbed my book bag to head out.

"I just don't even want to live right now," I heard someone say.

I turned around and it was Asia. At that moment it didn't matter how embarrassed I felt about my own family. Jeff's suicide tore us apart, and if I could help anybody know that was not the way to go, I had to say something.

I rushed over to her and said, "You can't do it."

Asia looked distraught. "You don't understand. Nobody cares about me. The girl I thought was my best friend has been laughing at me all over school. It's one lie told about me after another and nobody wants to be my friend. My mom is having problems with my stepdad and she's blaming me. I don't want to live anymore. Honestly, everybody's life will be better off if I just wasn't here at all."

"Asia," I said with empathy as I rubbed her back.

As the tears started to fall from her eyes, they started to fall from mine too. Why did life have to be so tough for us teens? What could I say to get her to see that it could get better?

I spoke from my heart. "You know that I know what this can do to a family. I can't bring my brother back. He was where you are, feeling like everything was too hard, and nothing would work out. Asia, my life hasn't been great since he's been gone. Things have been crazy for us too. My mom has been trying to hold down more than one job, I don't have any girlfriends, and my brothers can't get along. It's just one thing after another with me as well. I'm always talking to God and it seems like He's not fixing it quick enough, but then I make it to another day and I know it had to be only Him helping to get me through."

"But He's not helping me though, Yas. Okay? At least not down here anyway."

"If I could see my brother, I would tell him that we love him— that all the things that he thought were too hard could be overcome. If he would just give them to God, they wouldn't have been such a heavy burden. But I didn't know that's what he was thinking. I didn't know that's what he was going to do. But I can say to you, Asia, and anyone out here who's thinking the exact same thing, you might make mistakes, you might mess up, you might feel like you have nobody, but God is there. People are human. People are not perfect, but God is, and He loves you and can make it okay.

You just gotta keep believing and don't give up hope. Your family would be devastated."

"You might not think that they care," Miss Bennett came over and said to Asia, "but they love you, girl."

"And the LIGHT sisters love you too," Mrs. Newman said, beckoning all of us to come over and hug Asia.

"I know that it wasn't easy for Yasmin to open up and talk about how suicide affected her family, but if we learn from each other and help one another be better and stronger and get through stuff, then we're not going through all this in vain. Anyone else who wants to talk to me about it, I'm here. Does anyone else need to talk to Yasmin?" Miss Bennett asked.

Several hands went up, including Veida's. At that moment, I knew I had gone through something severe, but God was going to help me deal with it because I had to be strong for people other than me.

Chapter 9

Deeper
Sadness Prevailed

Girl, what did you do to Ma?" Yancy asked as I came into the house on Saturday from visiting the library.

"What are you talking about? I haven't done anything to Ma. I've been doing everything right, okay?"

He said, "She just told that modeling lady that you can't take lessons."

"What? That was last year and it wasn't lessons, it was one class. The lady called back to give me another modeling job?"

"I don't know about all of that. I just heard it was some big class for six weeks and you wouldn't even have to pay nothing and Ma just turned it down."

Yancy loved getting under my skin. However, the serious way he was looking at me, even though he didn't know how hurt I was by the news he was giving me, I could tell he wasn't playing.

I quickly burst into the kitchen and said, "Ma, Yancy just said that Miss Hall called from the modeling agency. Is it true that she had a modeling scholarship for me and you said no? Ma, please tell me this isn't true."

With her hand on her hip, she said, "Yasmin, don't come in here with all of that yelling and drama."

"But, Ma, it can't be true. You told me last year that I couldn't do it because my grades weren't good and I understood, but that's not the case now. I've been working hard and I've been pulling my weight. Why can't I have something that I want to try? Why can't you support me in my dream? I can't believe you didn't even talk to me before you decided to tell her no. Don't I matter? Don't I count? Isn't it my life?"

"Yasmin, please! First of all, I have no way of picking you up and you hadn't even mentioned modeling recently. And another thing, it's only been a couple of months of good grades out of you young lady, and I just don't think that's enough time to make sure you're completely focused."

"So, you just want me to come home every day when I don't meet with my LIGHT group? How come I can't have something else positive to put into my life?"

Never had I ever walked away from my mom, but the only thing I had been thinking about that was exciting was being up on the runway strutting my stuff and feeling confident about who I am. It's fun to make other people excited about the way I can work a garment. No disrespect to her, but the only thing I could do was run, put my head on my pillow, and cry.

Surprisingly, Mom didn't come into our room all domineering. She came over, sat on the side of the bed, and rubbed my back. She must have understood what I had said.

In a sweet tone, she said, "Yasmin, I know how much this

means to you, baby. This modeling business is hard work, and a lot of those girls do crazy things to their bodies just to try and please people. I don't want you to get so caught up in your looks that you don't try to put nothin' in your head."

"Just like Jeff liked basketball, I guess I found my passion in modeling," I explained to her.

"Yasmin, I have never seen you want something so bad that it stirs you all up on the inside and you storm away from me like that. You were so worked up you couldn't even talk about it. I know you're growing up, baby, and I don't want you to think that I don't care about your dreams. As long as you can show me that you're responsible, you can take the modeling classes."

"For real, Ma? Are you serious?" Excitement flooded me and I felt like I could breathe again.

"Yeah, but if you don't do what I expect, the classes stop. You understand?"

"Yes, ma'am. Thank you!" I said, hugging her so tightly I couldn't possibly squeeze any harder.

⪼⪻

For the next four days, I couldn't even sleep. When Wednesday came and I went to modeling practice, I felt like a soda can that had been shaken up and ready to pop.

That was until I got there and saw Veida staring back at me. But I got up on that runway, followed Miss Hall's instructions, and did my thing. I wasn't going to let Veida ruin my time in class, but then she got up to walk and she stumbled. A couple of the other girls laughed.

"I can't do this! Forget it. I don't even know why I tried," she cried, dashing to the bathroom.

I was standing there at a crossroads. Clearly something was going on with her. Something had shaken her up and gotten her upset. Just a week ago I stood before a group of girls, including Veida, at the LIGHT meeting. I had really tried to encourage them.

I just kept thinking about Jeff and him not having anybody to talk to. As mad as I was, I would be even madder at myself if anything else happened to her because I was too stubborn to be there for her. I had to be the difference—or at least try.

When I knocked on the door, she said, "I'm in here; just give me a second, please!"

"Veida, it's me, Yasmin."

She opened the door. "You don't want to talk to me. You get up there with all of those good moves, and I don't even know why I'm here. I'm too short for modeling. I don't care anyway," Veida sounded very distressed.

"That is absolutely crazy talk. You know you care in a big way," I responded.

"You already told me you were never going to be my friend again, Yasmin."

"Veida, just forget about all of that right now. What's wrong? You're so strong and confident, but you're falling down on the stage you love so much. Talk to me."

"My mom thought I was staying after school a couple months back, but I came home early from tutoring and caught her getting cozy with some guy. She told me that I couldn't tell my dad because it would ruin our family. So when my old boyfriend called me, I did something stupid. I guess I was trying to be like my mom. I lost a good friend, though, a good guy who I cared about. I lost a part of myself too. My dad soon found out, and now my parents are in counseling and stuff. I don't know if we can ever be a family again."

How could I not hug her at that moment? Suddenly I understood so much about why she had been acting so crazy. It was never about me. She had true pain that I couldn't even begin to understand. I guess I wasn't the only one going through something. Maybe now we could help each other overcome our pain.

"Hey," I said into the receiver when I got home from modeling practice.

"Yasmin? Is that you?" Veida asked.

"Yeah, I just thought I'd check on you, Veida."

"You don't know how much it means to me that you called. I know I let you down in the worst way, but for you to cheer me up a couple of hours ago does so much for me. For you to take time to call me now . . . I mean, I didn't expect us to be friends anymore." Veida sounded so sincere.

I paused. I really didn't know how to respond to that. We both had so much going on, and Yancy felt that she'd broken his heart. How could I just move on like none of it made a difference? How could I not give her the grace that God gives me? She deserved the same forgiveness.

So I said, "Look Veida, you letting me in on everything that is going on with you tells me a lot. I understand you more."

"So you forgive me for all this stuff and the way I've been dealing with Yancy?"

"Yeah, I forgive you even though it's not the best feeling," I explained.

"Thanks, Yasmin. You just don't know how good you got it."

"Veida, what are you talking about? There is so much going wrong in my life too. Girl, the grass just looks greener. But trust me —mine is burnt."

Veida said, "Well, for you to call is a big deal."

"Well, I'll see you tomorrow at lunch," I said reassuringly.

"Yeah, that'll be good." She sounded all excited. "Yas?"

"Yeah, I'm here."

"How's Yancy doing?"

I couldn't tell her that my brother was a basket case and he had been sulking big time. The girl didn't know that she'd hurt him that bad. However, I couldn't blow off the whole thing either. I was dumbfounded.

"Yeah, I really messed up, huh?" she said, when I gave no response.

Being honest, I said, "Just take care of you and I will try to take care of him, cool?"

"Thanks, Yasmin," she said, laughing a bit.

⚜

Then there was a knock at the door. It was Randi from next door. "Yasmin, I'm hungry."

"Randi, did you ask your mommy to give you something to eat?"

"My mommy won't wake up."

"What do you mean?" Then I realized that I was talking to a five-year-old. I yelled out to Yancy that I would be right back. He mumbled something and I went next door.

Randi was not exaggerating. Her mom was passed out on the couch. I went and checked on Dante and he was asleep. I tried to wake Miss Sandra, but I had no success. I saw a beer bottle lying next to her. It was the middle of the day.

"You didn't have any of this, did you?" I asked Randi.

She picked it up and handed it to me. "No, 'cause it was all gone."

I didn't know what to do, but I couldn't leave the kids there with their mom not responding. Pacing and watching her, I stayed a couple of minutes and decided if she didn't move soon that I was gonna call 911. Finally, I noticed a jerking movement. I then realized that she would be okay. I wrote a note: *Got Randi and Dante next door with me. Yasmin Peace.*

An hour later my mom came home and the first thing she said was, "Are you kidding? Miss Sandra dropped these kids over here on a school night?"

"No, Randi came over and got me." I said.

I got up and went over to Mom and whispered, "Ma, I think she's drunk."

"I gave her so many chances. This is ridiculous. This is not gonna be on my hands anymore." My mom was about to go off.

She went to the kitchen, grabbed the phone book, and started flipping pages. I could tell whatever she was about to do she wasn't totally comfortable with it.

"Yes, I need to report a child neglect case."

"Ma, you can't." I tried to grab the phone.

She turned away and said, "I told her the next time I was going to have to step in."

As Mom waited to talk to a social worker, I held Dante. He just thought I was cuddling and playing with him. He had no idea about what was happening.

Then there was a bang at the door. The knocks got louder. I knew it was Miss Sandra.

"Let me in! I need to get my children," she said.

"Mommy," Randi said, running to the door.

Mom opened the door and she and Miss Sandra gave each other tough stares. The tension was so thick that a knife could not cut it. I didn't dare move or speak.

"What's going on, Yvette? What you doin' on the phone?" Miss Sandra asked, looking at my mom with the Yellow Pages in her hand.

"Your kids need to stay here now," Mom said, shooing her away.

"Oh, no they not! These are my kids and I'm taking them with me. I wish somebody would come over to my house talkin' 'bout they taking my kids. I can't believe you. And I thought you were a neighbor who cared."

"I thought you were a mother who cared," Mom shot back.

Randi started crying, so Dante did too. Miss Sandra took both of her kids, slammed the door, and went back home. My mom just hung up on the social worker without giving all of the information.

Mom prayed, "Lord, this is hard. I'm just trying to do the right thing by those kids. I don't want to betray her either. Lord, please just help her. Help me to help her. I hate seeing her falling apart. If something happens to them, though, I'll never forgive myself. Only You can fix this. Amen." Mom was slightly bent down from frustration.

Trying to comfort her, I said, "They're going to be okay, Ma, they are."

"I hope so, Yas. Goodness, I hope so," she said, holding me tightly.

⟨⟨❦⟩⟩

I couldn't help but think, *Okay Lord, this is my eighth-grade field trip and I'm on a bus sitting alone.*

The ride to St. Augustine, Florida, was only about forty-five minutes. However, hearing all of the laughter in the background and not being a part of it, truly got under my skin. Veida was on the first bus, my brothers and Myrek were on the second, and I was on the third. To make things worse, before I could get into my personal pity party, I heard Perlicia's big mouth.

Perlicia vented, "Asia, I'm sick and tired of you anyway, always thinking you better than people. Ain't no need in rollin' your eyes and tellin' me I'm wrong to talk about people. If the girl smells nasty, then she just stinks. She better put on some perfume, soap, or something."

Asia said, "It's not cool to just hurt people's feelings. That's all I'm saying."

"What? You think they might try and hurt themselves like you did the other day?" Perlicia asked.

I couldn't just sit there in my own world anymore. Perlicia had practically turned into a bully. I got up out of my seat, went back a couple of rows, and got up in her face. "You love talking about everybody else, calling them out, trying to make them less of a person. If I wanted to, I could do the same thing to you."

"Trust me, Yasmin Peace, who's scared to kiss a boy, so po' you share a bed with yo' momma, and you ain't got no daddy 'cause he locked up in jail. You don't want to try and call me out!" She put her hand in my face.

"You know what? Forget it. You ain't even worth it," I said, feeling clobbered as I heard the crowd roar. Yet, I tried hard not to stoop down to her level.

When we got to St. Augustine, the tour guide boarded our bus and started explaining the history of the city. Though social studies was one of my favorite subjects and I loved learning about geography and the past, Perlicia's comments prevented me from focusing. I considered myself a confident young lady. I was tall in stature and always walked with my head held high. Even though I did live in the projects, I was proud.

But in the big scheme of things, what did I really have going on? I was from a single-parent home. My family didn't even have enough money to go to fast food restaurants, and I always seemed to have some friendship drama. When we walked into the church, I just felt myself slipping back into a place where I wanted more than I had, where I didn't measure up.

I wanted to stay down. However, as I took in the magnificent beauty of the old church, the Lord made me aware that when you feel down and think you are having it bad, someone is having it worse. I saw Asia crying over in the corner.

I went to her and said, "I know you may want your space, but I was just trying to see if maybe you wanted to talk. Do you mind my company?"

Because she didn't respond and just looked away, I walked away. She didn't have to tell me twice. I knew how it was when you're going through something, and sometimes you just need to deal with it by yourself before you can share it with someone. We were in church, after all. Maybe she just wanted to talk to God.

"Yasmin, come back, please," she said surprising me.

"Asia, I don't mean to be pushy or anything, but what's going on? I heard Perlicia on the bus talking about you doing something to yourself?"

Then she pulled up her sleeve and showed me her wrist. It had a slit across it. I almost choked.

"It actually made me feel good when I did that. It's called a blood rush. I found out about it on the Internet. A lot of kids are doing it now to either get excited or to numb the pain of their lives."

This was a perfect example of why our parents, teachers, and counselors were always warning us about the dangers of the Internet.

"Are you serious?" I asked, not wanting to make her feel worse than she already did. "I thought we talked about not giving up in our LIGHT meeting."

"This won't kill you," Asia said.

"So you *think*. It's dangerous."

She said, "You just don't understand what's going on. My mom hates my guts."

"What are you talking about? I know you said your parents were having some problems."

"He's not even my real dad, he's my stepdad and he's been . . ."

She couldn't even go on to tell me what was all bottled up inside, but the only thing I could think of was disgusting. I just grabbed her hand and held it tight.

"You've got to talk to your mom about this!"

"Don't you understand? I've tried to and she doesn't believe me.

She just thinks I'm trying to break up her marriage. She hates me. She wants me out of the house. It's spring break next week and I've got to leave. Most of my relatives are in Alabama. I do have a cousin here but I don't know if she would understand.

"We came here a few years ago because my stepdad got a job with Perlicia's dad. The girl that I thought was my best friend. Now I have no one and as much as I try to be strong, I just keep breaking. Does God care about me, Yasmin? Is He there? Is He going to do anything? He knows the truth. And Lord knows I'd rather be anywhere than in that house with that man. But where am I supposed to go?"

I so wanted to give her answers, but hearing all of this messed up my mind pretty bad. I knew no adult was perfect, but for one to misuse a child? Though I wanted to give her encouraging news and tell her everything was going to be okay—I couldn't. I was right there with her, wanting God to show up more, tired of always having to take the back seat, feeling like life wouldn't get any better. Yes, deeper sadness prevailed.

Chapter 10

Your
Own Fault

Yasmin, York, and Yancy! Y'all get in this kitchen right now!" Mom screamed at the top of her lungs. I didn't know about my brothers, but I certainly hated it. And here we were, our first day off, and she was getting us up at the crack of dawn.

"Yes, ma'am?" I answered in a disgruntled tone.

"York, Yancy, don't have me keep calling y'all six and seven times before you boys move. Get up! I am so tired of y'all breaking stuff around here," she said as she walked over to the dishwasher.

"Now one of y'all did something to it 'cause it's not starting. I don't know what goes on when I'm not here. I told y'all to be careful when you use it 'cause it's old. But tell me if you mess it up so I can get the management to fix it. Y'all don't need to be using the dishwasher anyway. Ain't nothin' wrong with your two hands."

"I didn't do nothing, Ma," York said as he turned away and walked toward the room.

She snatched him back and said, "Boy, did I tell you to leave?

I am not even close to being done with you. See, that's your problem, you think you are too grown up to be disciplined. So I guess
ain't nobody touched it."

"Ma, I admit I need to pick up more around the house, but I
didn't touch the dishwasher," Yancy said, trying the sweeter ap-
proach. "I promise."

"Ma, I do clean up around here," I said, "So it wasn't me either."

"Well, maybe Mike can come over here and look at it," Mom
replied.

"Ma, I can take a look at it," York said.

He was such a trip. He just didn't want Mom to call Myrek's
dad. But Jeff had taught him how to use tools.

"And what do you know about fixing stuff?" Mom asked.

"I been learning to fix on cars. I'm in shop, remember? Plus,
Jeff schooled me."

"Okay," she said, feeling bad that she had questioned his skills.
"Don't make it worse than it is."

Mom worked so hard, she deserved a break. Every night she
came in and told me that she wanted me to stay in school so I
wouldn't have to end up with dead-end jobs. I was just happy she
loved us so much. She seemed so stressed.

York said, "All right, Yancy, I'm going to need you to grab a
monkey wrench."

"What's that?" Yancy asked.

"Boy, sometimes you have your head too far up in those books
that you have no common sense," Mom teased, smiling at Yancy.

York asked, "Yasmin, can you turn on the light? It's a little dark
in here."

Hoping York could fix the appliance, I quickly complied with his request and flipped on the switch. I was stunned when none of the lights came on. It wasn't dark in our apartment, but there certainly was no light. I guess my brain comprehended everything before I could say anything.

"The lights are not working either," Mom said. "Yas, try turning them on again."

So that she could see me flip the switch, I did it again.

"This is all on me," Mom said in despair.

She pushed the microwave buttons and it did not come on. She opened the refrigerator and it was dark. She left the kitchen, went into the hallway, and flipped the light switches. They didn't come on either.

"So the dishwasher's not broken," she uttered in frustration.

"But, Ma, you have been working," I said.

"I know, but I've been behind. I guess I thought they would give me a little bit more time before they would cut us off."

Mom just sat at the kitchen table and wept. The three of us stood there around her. We didn't know what we were gonna do. All her money went to pay bills. She was doing as much as she could. It wasn't her fault that she was so far behind that she couldn't catch up. We didn't have an outrageous lifestyle. We had no amenities or extras. We barely had the basics.

"Ma," Yancy said, "we just have to call Uncle John. He'll send money to help right away."

"No, if Daddy calls us we can tell him," York yelled out.

Yancy teased, "And what is he going to be able to do from jail, tell the warden to pay up?"

York went over and yanked Yancy by his collar. His eyes were so red with anger. With all we were dealing with, why couldn't they grow up and get over the drama?

Mom cried out, "Now, you guys need to stop. It's enough that we have to deal with this. We not askin' nobody for help. This isn't supposed to be happening to me. I'm so far behind I can't get ahead. Lord, help us."

I asked, "Ma, what about Mrs. Newman?"

"What about her?" Mom asked.

I said, "Well, not just her, but the church. They brought over food that one time and said they didn't mind helping us get on our feet."

With a stern face, Mom said, "I am not going to bother them. This is not an emergency!"

"Ma, if we don't have any electricity, it's an emergency," York said.

"Ma, if we can't go to the church for help, then it's hopeless," I said. "All of that praying you've been doing is for nothing. All of the reading of the Lord's Word. The church will help if you let them. So what's the harm in asking?"

"Yasmin, you are such a smart girl, but what you don't get is that I did this to us with my poor choices along the way. Nobody's trying to give me a handout." Her weeping intensified.

"Ma, you can't cry over this stuff," Yancy said. "I mean no disrespect."

"He's right, Ma," York said, surprising both my brother and me. "You can't keep beating yourself up for what's in the past."

She wiped her face and said, "All of that mail right there, I don't even open some of it because I know they asking for money that I ain't got."

"Like Dad said, Ma, you've got to live up to your mistakes and do the best you can. God knows how hard you're trying."

My mom stood up and hugged me. "Yeah, your dad is paying for his mistakes now and God can work this out."

I said, "Ma, it makes me think about that song that we sing at church, 'Jesus Can Work it Out.' You know how it says, *how you gon' pay your rent when all your money's spent, baby needs a pair of shoes, and you got a light bill due?*"

She made a call to the church. Hours later, the lights were back on. Literally and figuratively our lives were brighter.

⋘⋙

Mom and I sat up late into the night having one of our "girl talks." I told her about some of the stuff we'd been talking about in the LIGHT group. Just as we realized how late it was and were heading to bed, there was a banging on our front door. I just knew it was little Randi next door. When Mom opened it up, Asia stood there sobbing.

She frantically said, "Hi, Miss Peace. I'm Asia."

I stood next to Mom, unable to speak.

"What are you doing out this time of the night?" Mom asked her, letting her into our apartment.

"I'm sorry it's so late at night, but my mom said I had to get out of her house and I . . . I didn't know where else to go."

"Wait a minute, who is that at this time in the morning?" York asked.

"York, go back to bed. Everything's okay," Mom said.

Then she saw Asia's face and quickly went over and hugged her. Although my mother didn't know Asia, she felt for her. God was working because Asia didn't need to be out on the streets.

"Yasmin, go get us some water, girl."

"Yes, ma'am." I said.

I heard Asia explain. "I've been having problems with my mom for awhile. It's my stepfather and things have gotten out of control. My mom won't believe me about the stuff he's done and she kicked me out when I told her. She chose him over me."

Mom listened to Asia as she explained everything. I didn't even know the details of everything that was going on in her house. When Asia wouldn't stop crying, my mom just held her.

Then Mom prayed, "Lord, sometimes in this life, we just don't know how we are going to make it, but You say that we can come to You and trust and know that You will take care of us. Right now, I lift up this precious, sweet girl whose heart is broken. Why You allowed her to come to my house, only You know, Lord, but I pray that You can help me and Yasmin lighten her load. We're supposed to be our brother's keeper. I also pray for Asia's mother because I know she must be sick and worried about where her daughter is. We love you, Lord, in Jesus' name Amen."

"My mom doesn't care where I am." Asia tugged away without saying Amen.

"Honey, you can easily say that because you are not a mom. Let me have a one-on-one talk with her, and I bet we can figure this whole thing out."

"You don't want to do that. She is so angry with me. She just believes what he says. She says that I am ruining her marriage. Even if she wanted me back, I don't want to be there anymore . . . not while he's there." Asia started to shake, thinking about it all.

"Ma, she's scared. Can't you see?" I said as she went to the telephone to try and rectify things.

I guess that is where I got it from, but sometimes, we just can't fix everything. Asia had already told me that her mom was crazy. Sometimes parents couldn't see that they were too harsh or that they did some stuff wrong. But, of course, being a child in my mom's house, I couldn't tell her that.

"Give me the number, honey, and let me try and call your mom, please. You gotta understand that with all these crazy people out here, she could be worried sick. Plus, you left in the middle of the night and if they call the police and they find you at my house then . . . give me your number." My mom was stressed.

Reluctantly, Asia gave her the phone number.

"I was just calling," my mother said to Asia's mother, "to let you know that Asia is over here and . . . I'm sorry . . . what did you say?"

I couldn't hear the conversation, but I could tell from Mom's facial expressions that Asia's mom wasn't saying things that a worried parent would say when their child is in distress. She was rolling her eyes as she listened to Asia's mom.

When she hung up the phone, she said, "We are going to figure this out. You're right, your mom and me are at different places in our lives right now. I want you to get some sleep and we'll figure this out in the morning."

My mom hugged Asia and went back into our room. Asia looked nervous and jittery and said maybe she should leave.

I touched her shoulder to calm her and said, "Please don't leave. If my mom says she can help you, then she can."

"Your mom thought she could talk my mom into wanting me

back. That didn't work, did it?"

"Obviously, our moms are a little different. Though my mom ain't got all of the answers, at least she is willing to try, okay?"

"You just don't know how blessed you are," Asia said.

I didn't really feel all that blessed because there was so much more I wanted and didn't have. I longed for my dad to be out of jail and my oldest brother to be alive. I wished we had money so we wouldn't have to worry about our lights ever being turned off again. But I knew Asia was speaking of something completely different. A part of her innocence was gone and she felt like it was her fault. Her mom was telling her that it was her fault. I couldn't leave her that night. As she lay down and finally drifted off to sleep, I just kept praying for God to turn things around in her broken life.

The next morning, we woke up to bacon and eggs. Mom threw down in the kitchen. Asia dashed off to the bathroom when York and Yancy strolled into the family room and she thought she looked a mess.

"I forgot you had brothers. Two fine brothers at that," she said, after finally letting me in the bathroom.

"Here, wash your face with this. My brothers see my yucky face every morning. Trust me, they're only awake after they get something in their stomachs."

After Mom talked to Asia for a long time about her family, she discovered that she had a cousin who lived in our apartment complex. Asia explained that she thought about going there but feared that her cousin would make her go back home. Her cousin, Roxanne, was twenty-seven-years old and married with a baby. My brothers knew her husband, so they went and got her. She came over and talked to us.

"Girl, you know you can come and stay with me. If our grandma in heaven could see us and I wasn't helping you, she would go off on me."

Asia hugged her cousin.

Asia said to my mother, "You just don't know how much it means that you care, and you're not even family. I wish my mom felt the same way."

"Well, sweetheart, you can't worry about that right now. Focus on what you can control. God's got you. I'm praying that things will work out, and we'll let your mom know where you're staying. Even though I'm not family, I'm thankful that God allowed me to be available for you."

Roxanne said, "Oh, I'm going to call my auntie too; she knows Asia wouldn't lie about something like this. Thanks for being there for Asia."

"No problem, I'd want somebody to be there for my daughter in a situation like this," my mom told Roxanne.

"Thank you, Yasmin," Asia said, "you're a great friend."

For the first time in a long time, I really felt like I was. That feeling felt good. Helping others really took the stress off my life's drama.

❦

Spring break flew by, but I was happy to be sitting at lunch with Asia and Veida. Both of them had been going through a lot personally, and because I found a way to put our differences in the past, I was able to help them move on.

"You know my mom still hasn't called me," Asia said as we both bit into our hamburgers. "Your mom told her where I was, didn't she?"

"Yep."

"So did my cousin, but she said that she didn't care. She won't even let me come and get my stuff."

"Parents are crazy, girl," Veida chimed in. "My mom said that my dad took better care of his law practice than he did her and then he found out that she had been looking elsewhere. I don't know if he is ever going to forgive her."

"Not knowing how to deal with it in the right way has made me do some stupid things," Veida said.

"Wait, there's Yancy. Yasmin, do you think he'll talk to me?" Veida asked. My brother and a group of guys were walking through the cafeteria headed back to class.

"I don't know, Veida, you may just want to leave that alone."

"No, I've got to talk to him."

"Veida, If I were you . . . "

Before I could get through to her, she had dashed over into my brother's face. He walked the other way when he saw her coming. I so hoped she'd get the point, but she didn't.

"What do you want?" my brother asked loudly.

"I just want to talk to you in private, please? Can we go some-where?"

There were like four or five guys around him. All it took was one to reveal the fact that everyone knew Veida was in some other guy's face. Peer pressure in middle school was fierce.

One dude pushed my brother toward her and said, "What you gon' do, man? You gon' listen to this sob story? I know you ain't that much of a punk. She played you!"

"Don't listen to them, Yancy. Please? I am sorry," Veida pleaded.

"You should have thought about that a long time ago. You lost a good thing. You should hurt."

Yancy walked away with his wannabe cool posse. He just left her standing there. I went right over to Veida, but she jetted to the bathroom.

As we walked from the cafeteria, Asia said, "You told her she needed to leave it alone."

"Yeah, I know, I just feel bad for her though," I said in a huff.

"You are a good friend, girl. It's all over school about how she dogged him. That's on her. He really wouldn't have no reputation if he took her back."

"Yeah, but I live with him and I know he still cares for her," I explained. "Sometimes we just make mistakes, and we need those that really care to look past that."

Later that afternoon as we got on the bus, Asia was still feeling hurt over her situation. "I guess you can't live past everything. I am living it right now. My mom won't even talk to me." I felt so sorry for her but the more I thought about it, I didn't have any words that would instantly make it better.

⁂

It was the first time Myrek was riding the bus in a while. Basketball season was over. After we got off the bus, I just walked up to him as he started down the street.

I said, "Hey, I know that you said we just need to leave each other alone, but how can I do that? You're my buddy. I miss our talks. I don't want there to be so much animosity between us."

Furious, he asked, "What do you want me to say, Yasmin?"

I answered, "Say that we can be friends. Say that you care about me too. Say that we can figure this out. Say something."

He looked back at me, rolled his eyes, and walked home faster. My heart pounded. I had lost my best bud. This was hard.

"I told you that boy don't want no friendship thang," York said. He was all up in my business as he and Yancy caught up to me walking home.

I took my fist and jabbed him in his side. "Who asked you?"

Just as we reached the apartment complex, Myrek was getting in the car with his dad. As they backed out of the driveway, Yancy started shouting, "Watch out! Watch out!"

At first, I didn't see little Randi. She was rushing up to grab her little brother's hand. Myrek's dad quickly swerved to avoid hitting them. My heart stopped. This was crazy. I hurried to grab Randi and Yancy grabbed Dante.

"Where's your mom, y'all can't be out in the streets like this!" Yancy asked with excitement. It was a pretty intense moment that had fortunately turned out okay.

"She had to go somewhere," was all little Randi could say.

"Their mom just left them home alone?" Mr. Mike asked, shaking his head. We all knew that it was time for somebody to do something.

❧

Hours later, DCF workers from the Department of Children and Family Services workers were interviewing Mr. Mike, my mom, me, and little Randi. There still was no sign of Miss Sandra. They left a note on the door for her and picked up both of the kids. It was hard because Dante was crying and Randi kept asking me to do something. I had been so opposed to DCF being there; it seemed like only someone's mom could take the best care of her own children. But if it wasn't one thing it was another going on over there. They needed to be looked after the right way, and maybe Miss Sandra wasn't in the best position to do that.

When they were gone, I went over to Mom and said, "This is so hard."

Mom said, "Yeah, and I tried to stay out of it. I really did stay out of it, but they came to my door and I had to tell the truth and give them the whole history. Sandra had chance after chance to get it right with those kids."

I had hoped she could get it together too. I just hope that I didn't expect too much. Three hours later, there was banging at our door.

"Open up. Open up, Yvette!"

Mom opened the door and Miss Sandra stood there with a note from DCF in her hand. She was not pleased.

"What is this? I step out for a couple of hours and you gon' call the 'po po' on me?"

I vented, "My mom didn't call nobody."

"I'm not talking to you. Hush!" she said harshly. "This is grown folk's business."

"That's just it, Sandra, you didn't take care of grown folk's business! Okay? Now you need to call those people if you want your kids back. Explain to them where you were when your son almost got run over today."

Miss Sandra swatted her hand in a spanking motion. "I'm goin' to get Randi. I told her she had to stay in the house."

"Your daughter was just trying to come out and say hi to the older kids coming home from school. I guess your baby just ran out into the street. You just can't expect kids that small to take care of themselves. I'm sorry, but I can't help you."

"But, my babies are gone. I've got to have my kids back. You don't understand, I've got to . . ."

"I'm praying for you. Call DCF in the morning, but tonight you need to think long and hard, because this is your own fault."

Chapter 11

Better
Not Bitter

The weekend was here. It was such a pretty spring day. Sitting on the porch, all I could think about was wishing Randi were home so we could play catch. Unfortunately, her mom hadn't been able to give the Department of Children and Family Services any kind of rational explanation that would allow her kids to come back home.

All I could do was pray that they were okay. I knew it had to be hard for Miss Sandra's kids to be away from their mom. They didn't know that their mom was doing all she could to get them back. We heard Miss Sandra crying the last few nights. She was really taking this hard.

Myrek came outside. Quickly, I got up to go inside. Not that he owned the entire porch or anything, but things sometimes still felt strange between us.

"Wait. Wait. Can I talk to you?" he said, completely shocking me.

I said, "Yeah, sure."

"I know I've been a jerk lately. My own pride has been holding me back from talking to you and letting you know that you really do mean something to me."

"I'm sorry that we're feeling two different things," I said, wanting him to know it was never my intention to hurt him. "If I've done anything to lead you on—"

Cutting me off, he said, "No. No. You haven't, Yasmin. It's just that knowing the way I feel about you, I can't imagine that I'm in this alone. And it just blows my mind that you don't want us to really hook up and stuff. I know what my dad said to me about the whole kissing incident and my feelings about you as we get older—but it's still hard."

"So, what are you saying, Myrek? Can we try to be friends again?"

"I don't know. The things I want from you haven't changed. I look at you and every day I get more and more attracted to you. Even when I'm mad at you, I like you. I don't want to be bummed out at you. I don't want to walk around upset, and I don't want you to go in the house when I come outside. Summer's almost here and we've always played together and enjoyed the hood, you know?"

"Yeah, I may try and spend some time with my grandma and cousins this summer," I offered.

Myrek didn't look happy to hear that. It was another awkward moment between us. Then he reached out his hand and I shook it. Even though I really didn't know what we were shaking on, I did it. At least it was a step in the right direction, and for that I was so thankful. But it went back to being weird after that. He looked around nervously. I did the same, not really knowing what to do next, and then I thought about his sister Jada.

So I asked, "How's everything at home with Jada being pregnant and all?"

"I don't even know. That's how I knew I needed to do something to change my attitude 'cause my whole house just seems on edge," he confessed.

"Is she home?"

"Yeah, she's home."

Myrek went inside to get his sister. When she came out, I couldn't believe how large she was. Though we lived next door to each other, I hadn't seen her in a while.

Myrek went back inside, thinking we wanted to be alone.

&

"Hey girl," I said, reaching out to give her a hug, but she sort of hugged me back weakly.

"I've got some news, Yasmin, and I don't know if your mom's gonna like it," Jada said.

I sat down in a chair and motioned for her to do the same. She sat and looked around. She was having difficulty telling me what was going on.

So I silently prayed, *Lord, I hope the baby is okay. Obviously this isn't good news. Help me to be able to deal with it.*

"I definitely decided that I'm not keeping the baby," she finally got the words out.

I didn't know how to react to that. A part of me clearly understood. I mean, she was young. To give up her whole life for a baby —to even ask her to do that—just seemed so unfair. But this was my niece or nephew. I knew my mom had been giving her maternity clothes, buying baby things from the thrift store, and making all these plans on how she was going to spoil her grandchild. But keeping it real, this wasn't my mom's decision.

"So, how does your dad feel about it?" I asked.

Jada said, "He thinks it's the right thing to do. I don't know if you guys noticed, but he's been home during the day. He got laid off."

"Are you serious?" I said as my mouth dropped, remembering I'd seen his car in the afternoon. I'd just never given it much thought.

I had no idea Myrek's family was coping with so much. Another mouth to feed would just add too much pressure. The Peace family needed to do all we could to help.

I said, "But we're right next door. We can keep the baby sometimes."

"If my baby is right next door, do you know how hard it's gonna be for me to stay away? Don't get me wrong, Yasmin, I love this child. And I know that even though I'm young, I loved your brother."

Asking the tough question, I said, "Have you found a family?"

"No, that's the problem. Everyone they show me isn't good enough. I've just been asking God to lead me to the family that needs to have this child. I haven't found them yet and I'm due in a couple of weeks."

"Do you know what you're having?" I asked.

"I didn't want to find out. I didn't want to get too close to the baby. Either way, I thought as much of this I could keep at a distance, the better. I know your mom's gonna hate me."

"She wants what's best for you, Jada, she really does. She could never hate you."

"You know I love this baby, right?" she asked me, almost as if she needed my approval. "What I'm doing is wrong, huh? I know that's what you think."

"No, no. I didn't say that. I don't know what I would do if I was in your shoes, Jada. But I know if you said you've been praying about it, God's leading you in a way that's right. Take your time, find the right parents, and if you change your mind, then you change your mind.

"You're already doing the right thing. You're allowing this baby to have a chance. We both have parents who struggle to take care of us, and my mom says that parents should want their children to have a better future than they had. I know I want my kids to have a good family, pretty clothes, and live anyplace other than the hood."

"Yeah, it's just so hard, Yasmin. Every time I think I'm making the right choice in giving the baby up for adoption, a part of me wants to keep this baby, but I know that I can't do anything for it. I wanna reach some of my dreams, but if I have a baby, if I'm a mom, I can't. Some days I resent this child. I know that's hard to say and I know that's wrong, but I have to be honest. I've been mad at God before. Top that one."

"Um. Get in line, me too. But He gives me grace, Jada. He cares for me. He cares for you and He cares for that baby. He's gonna help you figure out what's best."

"I believe He will too. Thank you, Yasmin."

I was so happy that I wasn't in her shoes. More girls needed to think of the consequences that young motherhood could bring—before they find themselves walking in those tough shoes. However, I know God can make something special out of our messes.

"It's like I hear Jeff talking through you," Jada said. "You're so wise, girl. You're ready for high school."

Finally, we hugged and this time it was as close to a bear hug as it could be, considering her stomach. Jada headed up the street for a light walk. Watching her, I could see the sun beaming down on her as if my brother was smiling from heaven. Things might not work out the way we want them to, but I knew deep in my heart that they were going to be okay for all those who lived in my world.

❧

The LIGHT meeting couldn't have come quickly enough for me and my friends. Posted outside the library was the sign "Self-Esteem Workshop." This was perfect. I'd been up and down lately and so had Asia. My life hadn't exactly been a bed of roses, so anyone who could give us advice on how to stay upbeat and not be in a funk was somebody that I certainly wanted to listen to.

"Nobody can help me," Veida said as she walked into the room full of books. "I'm a failure and beyond help."

I said, "Veida, don't be so dramatic about it, girl."

"I saw your brother earlier today and he wouldn't even talk to me."

"So! Don't base your life on what my brother does and does not do."

"You wouldn't even understand, Yasmin."

"What are you talking about?" I asked her.

"'Cause you got a boy who's crazy about you. But, girl, you don't even give him the time of day. You don't even understand why it feels sad when a boy ignores you."

"I know what it's like to be down and to feel like everything is your fault, and there's nothing that you're able to do to get it back right again," I said in a defensive tone. "I'm not trying to say that how you're feeling is not a big deal, Veida. I'm not. If I didn't care, I wouldn't be hanging out with you. But even I realize that we all make mistakes and we all just need to get better from them."

"Girls, come on in and sit down," Mrs. Newman said.

"Today, Miss Bennett and I are going to talk to you guys—so no special guests.

"You see from the poster board outside that our topic is self-esteem. A lot of you have really been down this semester, taking on the plight of the world in some cases. I know you feel like you have to be a savior and make everything okay."

That was certainly the case for me. I was thinking as I sat there listening that there had to be a way to keep happiness around me. I sat there waiting for Mrs. Newman to give us some hope.

"See, young ladies, it is not about wallowing in your pit of gloom. Life is never going to be perfect, and we can always have more, do more, get more, and be more, but it's about finding a way to enjoy what we have. Self-esteem is about being proud of who you are and how God made you. You have to get to a point in your life that no matter what happens you try to make the most of it. You know the saying 'when life gives you lemons, don't stay sour—make lemonade.'"

Perlicia raised her hand.

"Yes, Perlicia?" Miss Bennett said.

Perlicia said, "The problem is, some days I like myself and the other days I don't. Sometimes my hair will act right and then other days it's hideous to me. My clothes fit just cute and then some days

I hate my shape. I mean, self-esteem fluctuates for me. What am I supposed to do to keep it stable?"

Mrs. Newman said, "I will answer that. The first thing you have to do is not let everything hang on how you look, dear. You have to know that you're cute when your hair isn't acting right or when you don't look so model-like in an outfit. If you already know that every day isn't going to be perfect, then that can't dictate how you feel or respond. So you are already victorious. Know that you got it goin' on. Believe that within yourself. Don't be cocky about it, but start each day off feeling like life is going to be great."

"What if people you love weigh you down by turning their backs on you?" Asia started blurting out her questions. "What if they treat you as if you're nothing? Like they don't love you anymore or care, when their love is supposed to last you a lifetime? What are you supposed to do then? How are you supposed to feel about yourself?"

"If that happens," Miss Bennett said, "you know what, Asia, we can't control other people, even those who are close to us. Those we live with and those we trust with our hearts can let us down every now and then. But that doesn't mean that we have to let ourselves down by believing what's being said or by accepting their unfair treatment of us. Don't let anyone steal your joy, no matter if the people who are supposed to set great examples for you don't. Hold your head high."

"When you know the right and wrong thing to do," Mrs. Newman added, "then you have to make sure you do the right thing. We adults aren't perfect. We don't get it right all the time. We do expect you to do what we say, not what we do. If those who are supposed to be leading you let you down, you can't use them as a crutch or an excuse for you to do wrong. But even if you do mess up by following someone who led you astray, pick yourself up, dust yourself off, and reevaluate your own priorities."

I really liked that we could talk and get out those deep things that we were feeling. Life wasn't gonna be easy but we can control a lot of it. I couldn't exactly say what I was for sure going to do or how I would act the rest of my life, but I was definitely determined to look at things more positively, to believe that things would turn out okay, and know that God was ultimately in control. I realized that my being down wasn't ever going to help me get back up and walk on for Him.

Yeah, I had great self-esteem, I loved myself, and I wanted to get better. With that in mind, coupled with the fact that I adored my Creator, I had it going on. That was a great thing!

After the meeting, Asia approached Miss Bennett and Mrs. Newman and gave them more details about what she had been going through.

❧

Later on that day, I was searching for a bottle of nail polish on my dresser.

I heard Mom say, "No, I'm cool with it. If Jada wants to give up the baby, it's gonna break my heart, it's gonna be hard for me, but I'll respect that. I've been praying about it and that's just the right stance to take." She was talking on the phone to Big Mama and changing her clothes for work. "I don't know, Ma, I can't get all into the child's business. She's dealing with her dad and I'm just praying that somebody is gonna do right by my grandbaby.

"I gotta get on outta here and get to work. The kids are good.

Yasmin may come for the summer. Yes, Ma, I'm gonna make sure they call you. Yasmin is right here if you have a minute to holler at her. Okay, hold on. All right, love you too."

My mom handed me the phone and Big Mama said she couldn't wait to see me this summer. She had to hurry up and hang up too because she had to get to choir rehearsal.

After we hung up, I said to Mom, "So, you know, Ma?"

"What? About Jada and the baby?" she asked.

"Uh huh."

"Yeah, they talked to me, her and her dad. And quit listening to my conversations," she said, looking sad.

"I'm sorry, Ma. I know you wanted to be a part of the baby's life."

"Yeah, but she's a teenage girl. I certainly can't raise no more children. Not that my heart ain't big enough and not that the Lord won't make a way. It's just that for some reason I know He's got another plan. That sounds weird, huh?" she asked me.

"No, Ma, you just believe that God is in control and that He'll work it out His way. You're stepping aside, letting Him be God. That's very cool."

"Oh, so you been gettin' something from Sunday school since you've been going every week," she said smiling.

"Yeah, and the LIGHT meetings too. I just know that as long as we live the way He's called us to, study His Word, and do the best we can—He's got us—and it's all good. No need to stress, no need to worry, no need to be bummed out, just trust."

"I hear you, girl. You and your brothers please don't get into any mischief. I won't be home until later tonight. After I get off work, Mr. Mike is gonna pick me up and we're gonna go and get some ice cream. It's not a big deal at all, before you ask, Yasmin."

"That's cool, Ma. Enjoy and bring me somethin' back," I said smiling. "And I will keep your two sons in line. I promise."

It wasn't even eight o'clock and just a couple of hours since Mom had been gone when those two started fussing. I had absolutely no idea what it could be about. However, when I opened the door to their room, stuff was everywhere.

I screamed, "Why y'all always gotta do this? Why can't y'all just get along?"

"I'm sick of him. That's why," York said.

Yancy replied, "Whatever, you're the one who thinks you know everything."

"No, you the one that thinks just because you make good grades that I'm stupid as I don't know what," York rebutted.

"Whatever, boy," Yancy said.

York said, "I got your 'whatever.' You get out there in those streets and you wouldn't even be able to survive."

"That's why I'm trying to get something in my head so I don't have to be out in the streets, dummy."

"Okay, enough, y'all," I stepped up and said.

Yancy shouted, "I just hate him!"

"Why you gotta use such harsh words?" I asked Yancy.

Yancy said, "'Cause, Yasmin, this is real. That's how I feel."

"He ain't alone in feeling that. I hate you, too, so now what?" York said in a tougher tone.

"Guys, stop."

York walked down the hall. We followed him. I stayed by Yancy so no more drama could start. Then suddenly York's demeanor changed.

"Y'all smell that?" York asked.

Both Yancy and I sniffed the air. I coughed. It smelled like smoke.

"Yeah, somebody's burnin' somethin." I said.

Yancy jabbed, "I can't believe you can smell it. You're probably immune, with all that weed you and your partners have been smoking."

"See, I'm so sick and tired of you," York charged at him.

Then the two of them started at it again. The smoke was becoming stronger. I ran to open up the door and stepped out. Smoke was coming from under Miss Sandra's door.

"Y'all come here. This is serious," I yelled. "Something's not right over here."

I knocked on the door and it was hot. York and Yancy came and started pounding on the door too. We all panicked.

"We gotta call 911! Hurry up!" I yelled. "She's gotta be in there, y'all! Her car is here!"

Yancy got the phone and called. We knocked on Myrek's door and told him and Jada. Then we knocked on other neighbors' doors. We didn't know who was at home and who wasn't. Some of the neighbors ran out with us with cell phones in hand trying to call other neighbors and friends.

"Has anybody seen Miss Sandra lately?" York asked.

Everybody said no, except for Yancy.

"Last time I saw her was yesterday," Yancy said. "She was walking around like a zombie. Those kids still ain't back."

York reminded us, "I know she drinks a lot. She smokes too. She coulda went to sleep with a cigarette in her hand. Who knows what's going on? We got to get her out of there, y'all!"

"How we gonna do that? We have to wait for the fire department. Y'all, I see flames back there!" I said as I went to the side window.

"I gotta go in and get her!" York said.

"Boy, you are not going in there!" I shouted.

"Naw, bro', you can't go in there!" Yancy said.

"Somebody's got to get her out!" York hollered.

York went around the side and broke the window before anyone could stop him.

"He hasn't come out yet?" I asked before taking a deep breath. Only about ten seconds had passed but it seemed like a lifetime. And where was the fire department?

Yancy, Myrek, Jada, and I began praying. York had done a good thing. He went in there to try and save a life, certainly the Lord was going to take care of him.

Just then we heard the sirens and knew that help was on the way.

And then Yancy held me. "I don't know if he's going to be all right."

"Don't say that. Stay positive, Yancy," I said crying.

Clearly, I could see that my brother was upset as well. He said he hated York, just minutes before, but deep down I knew that wasn't the case. Now he knew it too. In the middle of a crisis we were trying to pull together, and we needed God's help.

I said, "We have to know He's going to come out of there all right. Things will get better, not bitter."

Chapter 12

Happier
Feelings Reign

his couldn't be happening. We couldn't be losing York. I just stood there frozen as tears trickled down my face. I knew the Lord knew what was best. But just thinking about that grim reality made me sick.

"The flames are getting higher!" I squealed.

It felt like the firemen were moving in slow motion or something. The crowd had grown larger and larger.

"I gotta call Dad!" Myrek said to Jada.

"Yeah, and tell him that York is still inside," Jada said as a paramedic took her to the side and gave her some water and a chair to sit in.

Then Yancy looked at me and we realized that we hadn't called our mom. We were glad that she was with Mr. Mike so that she wouldn't have to come home alone to what was happening.

"You guys need to step back and let us do our jobs," the fire chief said to Myrek, Yancy, and me.

Yancy said, "Use us, sir! We gotta help. My brother's in there!"

He said, "Son, calm down. Is it just him?"

"No, sir, Yancy said, "our neighbor, Miss Sandra, is in there too!"

He touched my brother's shoulder, "Okay, we need you to stay back. You'll make finding your brother harder if we have to go in there after you too. Am I clear?"

Jada tried to calm Yancy down. At first he seemed to be listening, but then he fell to the ground and started rocking back and forth as if he were some kind of zombie. This was just too much to bear. No word was coming from inside the blazing apartment before us and the fire had now spread to our place.

And then one of the firemen yelled out, "We hear voices! We hear voices!"

"They're gonna be okay," Myrek said as he hugged me.

"I hope you're right," I said.

All of a sudden I heard a wail that could've only come from my mom. She and Mr. Mike found us in the crowd.

She cried, "You guys are supposed to be together. York is in there! What happened? How could you guys let him go in there? My baby, Oh Lord, my baby!"

"Coming through, coming through," a fireman called out, carrying the limp body of Miss Sandra. "We need the paramedics!"

Mom rushed over to Miss Sandra. I went with her. I was so thankful she was alive. Unfortunately, her burnt body was horrifying to view.

Her face was so badly burnt it looked scary. The ambulance rushed off with her. Thankfully, another one was standing by.

"Get my son!" Mom screamed out.

So many people from the neighborhood were crying out too. This was serious. The firemen were able to put out the flames. But there was still no sign of York. I knew the longer he stayed in there, the worse it would be.

So I prayed again, *Lord, I'm trying to stay hopeful. I'm not gonna give up on You, but we need York here. You know we do. Lord, get all of the debris out of the way. Help the firemen find him. He needs to be rescued now, Lord. I know You're not through with him yet on this side of heaven.*

Myrek touched me and said, "Look!"

I opened my eyes and the firemen were carrying York out on a stretcher. His arm seemed to be disfigured and it was burned badly as well. The worst part though, was that he wasn't moving. My mom ran over to him, but one of the firemen tried to keep her back.

She screamed, "Is my son alive? You gotta tell me something! Is my son alive?"

"Yes, ma'am. He's serious. We've got to get him to the hospital."

"Thank you, Lord," she said, clapping her hands. I knew we'd just prayed the same prayer. She got in the ambulance with York and they were gone.

"Come on, kids. I'll take you guys and follow them," Myrek's dad said.

Though I didn't know much, I knew the Lord was capable of anything. I'd just witnessed a miracle. God had answered my prayers. York was still here and that was a blessing. I could only hope he would continue to pull through.

We'd been at the hospital for hours and no one had come out to tell us anything. Though I wished my dad could be here, I had to admit Mr. Mike was keeping my mom calm, and for that I was appreciative.

Finally, the doctor came out. "York Peace's parent or guardian here?"

"Yes. I'm his mother! I rode over here with him, but they wouldn't let me go back there."

"No ma'am, that's because we needed space to work on your son. But I've got great news."

"You do?" she said with hope and peace all over her face just from hearing that little part.

"His left arm and hand are broken with third degree burns on that same hand. He did regain consciousness, but he is sleeping now. He has a concussion. We still need to monitor him. We won't know the extent of the blunt blow to his head until he wakes up and begins talking to us. But until then, an initial CAT scan and X-ray show that everything looks okay."

My mom went over and hugged the doctor, practically giving him a football tackle. But he didn't blame her. Her baby was going to pull through.

"And my neighbor?" Mom asked.

"She's in a little worse shape. Though she's conscious, we had to give her medicine to sedate her. Her burns are extremely severe and they're all over her body. Your son is truly a hero. If she would have received the blows to the head that he took on her behalf, there's no way she'd be here right now. You should be proud of that young man."

"Doctor, I am. I'm gonna get him for going into a burning

apartment, though, but I'm mighty proud of him at the same time."

"I understand. Oftentimes people who save folks risk so much and make very unwise and dangerous decisions, but in the end that's why we call them heroes. Everyone isn't willing to take such a risk. Obviously, credit goes to you for how you've raised this young man. Risking his life to save someone else's says a great deal about his character. Hats off to you."

When York's doctor said that to my mom, I thought about how both York and the firemen risked their lives by going into the fire. There was a chance they could make it out alive and a chance that they wouldn't make it out. But Jesus didn't risk His life for us. He gave His life. He went to the cross knowing that death was sure. He would die but get up again in three days. I couldn't wait to get to church to share that with my Sunday school class. I believe that's what my Sunday school teacher called getting a revelation about God's Word.

"Bless you, doctor. Can we go back and see him?" Mom asked.

"I'll tell the nurse to let you guys know when he wakes up. But even at that time there can only be two visitors."

As the night went on, the hospital emergency room became packed with more supporters.

All of a sudden my uncle and his wife walked in with Big Mama. Very surprised to see our family, we hugged all of them.

"Uncle John!" Yancy asked, "How'd you find out?"

"Your mom called her mother and she wanted to be up here. Of course, I wanted to be here too."

"Ma'am, your son is awake," a nurse came and said.

"I know the doctor said only two of us, but I've got two children who are here. We've all been worried all night. My son who's injured and these two are triplets, and his grandma needs to come in."

"Yes, ma'am, that's fine. The two siblings and you, please go in. He's calling for Yancy."

My brother's face just lit up. He'd been down most of the night. Maybe our family could heal after all.

As soon as he opened the door, Yancy said, "York, I'm so happy you're alive."

In a weak tone, York said, "I'm happy I am too, bro'. In that fire, I just kept thinkin' that I wanted you to know that I don't hate you."

"I wanted to get in the fire to get you out and tell you the same thing." Yancy reached over and hugged York really tight.

"Thank you, Lord," Mom said.

She and I gave both my brothers a big kiss. I was so full of joy seeing my brother alive.

The nurse came in and worked on York. She told us we didn't have much time. My mom gave her a sister girl look as if to say, are you kidding?

"We ain't going nowhere. We staying right here," Mom said as she pulled up a chair. "Baby, that was so brave of you."

"Is Miss Sandra gonna be okay?" York asked.

Mom brushed his forehead. "Yes, but she's gonna have a long recovery. Thanks to you, she's gonna be okay, son."

"All right now, one of y'all better come on out, so I can come on in and see my grandbaby," Big Mama said, standing by the door.

I went over to York and said, "I love you. Thank you for not leaving us. And I'm proud of you too."

"I love you too, Yas. You're gonna have to put up with me a little while longer."

Then York said something else so meaningful. "When I was in that fire, for real I saw angels keeping the fire off of me. If God can do that, I know He can do anything. I'm done with all that negative, destructive stuff."

"York, that's deep. God really protected you," I said. "And to say that you're finished with the street life is cool." To hear York say that he knew that God was looking out for him was better than hearing that he was physically okay. Now I knew deep down he believed God in his heart.

"Big Mama, Uncle John, Aunt Lucinda, Mr. Mike, and Myrek are here," I said.

"Really?" York asked, sounding very surprised.

A lot of people care about you York, family and friends." I explained, "Mr. Mike brought all of us over here. He's really been there for our family. Maybe you should cut Ma some slack and allow her to get to know him and make a choice for herself."

"It's good to know a lot of people care," York said. "Tell my boy Myrek I said 'What up?'"

I just smiled as I exited the room. I was excited to tell my brother how much I cared about him and how proud I was. I think he really listened to me when I told him that sometimes he tried to control things that were out of his control. He needed to love without conditions.

"Ooh, Grandma's here to take care of you," Big Mama said with a huge smile on her face as I passed her.

❧

As soon as I stepped out into the hallway, Myrek was by the door, "So, is he really okay?"

I said, "Yeah. He wanted me to tell you 'What up' and he is really excited that you care."

"Yeah, I mean me and him been boys since forever . . . and going into a burning apartment is just crazy. Now that he came out of this, I'ma kill him," Myrek teased, obviously relieved that his buddy would be all right.

I grabbed Myrek's hand and said, "Thank you for caring about all of us. Coming through tonight let me know that life is short and we are going to stay best friends. You got it?"

"Yep, I hear you, Yasmin."

"Your mom okay, Yasmin?" Mr. Mike asked.

"Yes, sir. She's fine."

"You know, I'm not trying to take the place of your dad, or anything like that, right?"

"Yes, I know. Did you take Jada home?" I asked.

"No, she's out there talking to your uncle."

"Yeah, they got some exciting news," Myrek said to me.

I didn't understand what he meant. Myrek and his dad were smiling, though. I couldn't wait to hear some more pleasant words. Then Yancy came out.

Mom nodded. I held the door and Myrek and Mr. Mike went into the room. Mr. Mike wiped his brow. I knew he was nervous about seeing York.

Mom went over and kissed York on the forehead. "Now, you get you some rest." She left feeling much relief.

When I went into the waiting room, Mom was just crying. I dashed to her. What was it now? Miss Sandra? What?

"What's going on?" I let out a worried cry.

"Girl, everything is fine," she said, in a happy tone, as she pointed to Jada. "Yasmin, you're not gonna believe this news. They found parents for the baby."

"You have?" I asked Jada. "What, Mom, you know them or something?"

"Yes! It's Uncle John and Aunt Lucinda!"

"Oh, my goodness!" I said excitedly.

Aunt Lucinda couldn't even hold back the tears, "Yasmin, I wanted a baby for so long. To be able to raise one as part of this family is only a blessing from God."

"But, y'all gon be in Orlando. I'm never gonna get to see my grandchild," Mom said as some of the excitement left her voice.

"No, that's the other news. We're moving up here. The trucking company that I drive for has a branch in Jacksonville," Uncle John explained.

Jada said, "That's what made me say yes. The baby can still be here and I can see him or her sometime."

Uncle John said, "And until they get that apartment of yours straight, you guys are gonna come live with us, Yvette. My brother would have it no other way."

She turned and looked at Mr. Mike, "What about your place, Mike?"

"We're fine. My apartment just has a little smoke in it."

It just felt so good on the inside that things were working out in my life. My brothers had begun to appreciate each other again, and York was gonna recover from his accident. Uncle John promised my dad that now that he'd be living in Jacksonville near us, he'd keep an eye out on all of us. York said he was done with destructive behavior and now he'd have Uncle John to keep him in line. Myrek and I had vowed to keep working on our special friendship. And my brother Jeff's precious baby would have the perfect home. God was up there doing His part. I was so excited that my family understood that we had to do ours.

Eventually we're all gonna leave this world. It even happens to some people when they are young, like my brother Jeff. Now, we don't have to fear if we know that our name is written in the Lamb's Book of Life. York had accepted Christ when our family joined the church but now he'd been in his own fiery furnace like Shadrach, Meshach, and Abed-Nego. In both situations, they all walked out unscathed. York had an experience with God.

Things were coming together for the Peace family. I now knew for sure no matter how dark things seemed, I could never give up hope. Always having a belief in God is a blessing. I knew life would still be tough, but because He is taking care of me and my family—happier feelings reign!

Acknowledgments

*W*riting a story dealing with such tragedy isn't the easiest for me to do. However, this series has been very fulfilling for me. I've found that in the pain there is joy. In the hurt there is healing. And in the suffering God brings relief. So I kept writing, even when the storylines yank at my heart, because I wanted you to know God cares and life will get better.

You might feel it's easy for me to say believe in hope, when I had two wonderful parents and never knew instability in my adolescence. But I have spent many days rejoicing with young people who have found something good out of their bad circumstances. If God did it for them, He is the same God who will do it for you. Though you may be heavy-laden, Matthew 17:11 says the hope you have to believe in with a doubt is that God can carry your load.

Forever know the Lord has your back. Below is a special thanks to the people who have kept me believing in the hope that my writing is not in vain. For when you believe in hope, you will know having a positive outlook makes all the difference.

To my family, parents Dr. Franklin and Shirley Perry, Sr., brother, Dennis, and sister-in-law, Leslie, my mother-in-law, Ms. Ann and extended family, Rev. Walter and Marjorie Kimbrough, Bobby and Sarah Lundy, Antonio and Gloria London, Cedric and Nicole Smith, Harry and Nino Colon, and Brett and Loni Perriman, your constant encouragement has helped me believe I'm living out what I've been called to do.

To my publisher, Moody/Lift Every Voice, and especially Cynthia Ballenger, your getting behind this series has helped me believe that this message God has given me to share is powerful.

To my 8th grade friends, Veida Evans, Kimberly Brickhouse Monroe, Joy Barksdale Nixon, Jan Hatchett, Vickie Randall Davis, and especially Amber Jarrett, who left us too early (girl we miss you, but we know God needed you), your enduring friendships have helped me believe having a core group of friends who loves you is worth so much.

To my sorority, Delta Sigma Theta, especially our 24th National President, Cynthia Butler-McIntyre, your generous gesture of placing me on the National Arts and Letters Commission has helped me believe dreams really do come true. *(For nine years I've prayed and longed to serve. Young people, don't ever lose hope.)*

To my children, Dustyn Leon, Sydni Derek, and Sheldyn Ashli, your reliance on me helped me believe that God has blessed me to bless you.

To my husband, Derrick Moore, your devotion to our family has helped me believe and know not all fathers are absent, dead, or in jail.

To my readers, especially the ones who truly identify with this deep story, your wounded spirit has helped me believe that though you may have it rough right now look up, for your Help is on the way.

And to Jesus Christ, who gave His life for my sins, Your unselfish act on the cross has helped me believe one day I'll be with our Father.

Discussion
Questions

1. Yasmin Peace's family is just finding out that her deceased brother's pregnant teen ex-girlfriend is now having his baby. Do you feel the way the mother is insisting Jada has the baby is right? What are some ways to help people without being too pushy?

2. Veida, Asia, and Perlicia are talking about sex at school. Do you believe Yasmin's response of wanting to stay pure until marriage is the correct one? What does the Bible say about this?

3. An after-school mentoring group is formed. What things are brought up in the group discussion that help the girls think more responsibly? What are things you do to stay encouraged?

4. Yasmin's uncle stays with them when her mom goes out of town. Did it help her to talk to him about her insecurities? Who are people in your life that you feel you can talk to and get wise counsel from?

5. Myrek kisses Yasmin and she doesn't like it. Is she wrong to tell him how she feels? If your friend isn't helping you please God, how can you deal with that in a positive way?

6. Yasmin knows how much her brother York listens to their father. Do you think she was right to call her dad for help when she felt York was in too deep? Do you believe the Lord wants you to help people get out of trouble?

7. Yasmin and York catch Yancy's girl, Veida, with another guy. Do you think they handled that whole incident correctly? How can you protect the ones you love without hurting them?

8. In the LIGHT meeting teen suicide is discussed. Are you happy Yasmin held it together and shared from the heart? Do you think the tough things we go through can help someone else?

9. The little girl next door is being neglected. Do you think Yasmin is right to do all she can to help? What are ways you can help those in need?

10. Yasmin's mom doesn't have enough money to pay all the bills and the lights get turned off. Do you think a teen should be angry when their parents can't meet the family's basic needs? How can prayer change situations like this one?

11. The triplets smell smoke and go next door to help. Do you think any of them should have gone into the blazing apartment? What are other ways they could have helped?

12. The brothers have not been getting along throughout most of this book until the fire scene. Do you feel that Yancy felt bad about that in the end? How and why can tragedy unite us?

FINDING YOUR FAITH

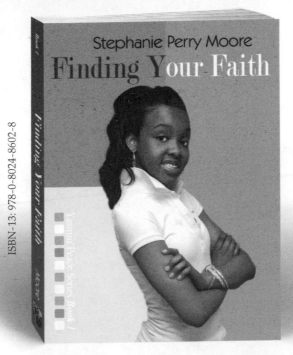

Yasmin Peace is growing up fast. After the tragic suicide of her oldest brother, she takes on the responsibility of overseeing what's left of her family and through it all, she perseveres. As she sheds her tomboy exterior and finds her faith, Yasmin blossoms into the young lady God destined her to become. Join Yasmin Peace on her journey through this series that will encourage character growth and development.

WWW.LIFTEVERYVOICEBOOKS.COM

1-800-678-8812 · MOODYPUBLISHERS.COM

THE PAYTON SKKY SERIES

From her senior year of high school to her second semester of college, this series traces the life of Payton Skky, showing how this lively and energetic teenager's faith is challenged as she faces tough issues.

The Negro National Anthem

Lift every voice and sing
Till earth and heaven ring,
Ring with the harmonies of Liberty;
Let our rejoicing rise
High as the listening skies,
Let it resound loud as the rolling sea.
Sing a song full of the faith that the dark past has taught us,
Sing a song full of the hope that the present has brought us,
Facing the rising sun of our new day begun
Let us march on till victory is won.

So begins the Black National Anthem, by James Weldon Johnson in 1900. Lift Every Voice is the name of the joint imprint of The Institute for Black Family Development and Moody Publishers.

Our vision is to advance the cause of Christ through publishing African-American Christians who educate, edify, and disciple Christians in the church community through quality books written for African Americans.

Since 1988, the Institute for Black Family Development, a 501(c)(3) non-profit Christian organization, has been providing training and technical assistance for churches and Christian organizations. The Institute for Black Family Development's goal is to become a premier trainer in leadership development, management, and strategic planning for pastors, ministers, volunteers, executives, and key staff members of churches and Christian organizations. To learn more about The Institute for Black Family Development write us at:

The Institute for Black Family Development
15151 Faust
Detroit, Michigan 48223

We hope you enjoy this book from Moody Publishers. Our goal is to provide high-quality, thought-provoking books and products that connect truth to your real needs and challenges. For more information on other books and products written and produced from a biblical perspective, go to www.moodypublishers.com or write to:

Moody Publishers/LEV
820 N. LaSalle Boulevard
Chicago, IL 60610
www.moodypublishers.com